TIME MARCHES OFF

by

Paul de Wreder

Original Cover by John Andrews

CONTENTS

TIME MARCHES OFF

by Paul de Wreder
(J. W. Heming)

CHAPTER ONE — AN INVITATION TO –

Billy Stewart stared at the card in his hand. "I don't believe it," he said positively.

"Neither do I," said Harry Nash. "But there it is in black and white."

"You've gone crazy now," said Billy. "This is silver and blue."

Harry sighed. "Just a figure of speech," he said. "Do I have to go into details, as to a little child?"

"Why not?" asked Billy.

Harry regarded Billy's 25 years of dumbness for a moment, then nodded. "Why not," he agreed.

Billy took another long look at the invitation. It was printed in silver on a blue card and respectfully invited them to a reception at Professor Slagoscar's mansion at Darling Point on Wednesday night.

Billy made a discovery. "It doesn't say who's getting the reception," he said. "Maybe it's us."

"If it's anything like some of the receptions we've been having lately I don't want any piece of it," said Harry.

"It says on the bottom R.S.V.P. Perhaps that's the joker."

"That means *repondez s'il vous plait*."

"Play what? I don't gamble—much."

"All right, let it pass. We won't be going anyway—we haven't anything to wear."

"Who cares? It might be fancy dress and we can both go as Adam. We've got to go. It says there'll be a supper."

"I said we're not going," Harry repeated. "Look at these clothes to attend a big reception. If I shave the threads off the bottom of these pants any more they'll be shorts."

"We're not going?" asked Billy.

"No."

"You're just a cad."

"I prefer to be called a twirp if it's all the same to you," Harry said. "And that's gratitude, that is. After me adopting you in Tobruk in 1941 and looking after you like a mother ever since."

"Yes—and why did you adopt me in that bomb shelter?" Billy asked. "Just because I'd managed to scrounge a bottle of beer and two sausages. That's why. And who helped me spend my money after the war? Eh, answer that?"

"You helped me spend mine when yours was gone," Harry said.

"You're just a waster," Billy said. "Here it is 1945 and what have you done since the war ended? Nothing. And I've had to scrounge for both of us. And here's a chance for a good supper and you turn it down. Flash, that's what you are!"

* * *

"There are the particulars of the two men I have picked out for the experiment, Mr. de Wreder," Professor Slagoscar said to me, handing me some papers. "One of my assistants hunted them up for me and I think they will serve the purpose very well."

I took the papers and glanced over them. To me had fallen the task of chronicling the adventures of the time-travellers—if there happened to be any adventures. I had my doubts. I was wrong, as this book proves.

"William Stewart," I read. "Age 25. Fought in the Second Great War and was decorated. Rather slow-witted, but not too slow. Has courage."

"Harry Nash. Age 28. Also decorated in Second World War. The smarter of the two. Has courage for the job. Both the men have gone through their money and are out of work. Live in a cheap boarding-house in North Sydney, the rent of which is three weeks behind. Neither has any relatives."

I passed the papers back to the Professor.

"The point is," I remarked, "whether they will agree to be the subjects of your experiment."

Professor Slagoscar chuckled. "I am taking no risks of that. I will inveigle them into the tubes and explain to them afterwards."

"But there may not be an afterwards," I protested. "What if they die?"

"There is no chance of that," the Professor said. "Now, as you are the author who shall give the results of my experiment to the world you had better have these particulars. Now— scientific details."

"The public don't want those," I remarked, with pencil poised over paper. "Keep those for the writer who is supplying the scientific journals. Just give me an outline."

"Very well. I have constructed two cylinders of glass and, with the aid of some knowledge I obtained from the Yogi I have mixed a potion. The cylinders are part of an intricate machine and with the aid of these and the potion, to put it simply, I believe I possess the means of transporting a man thousands of years forward through time. The subject vanishes, although staying in the same position, but is travelling so fast that it is impossible for mortal eye to see him. It is a sort of suspended animation, but during that suspension time races ahead, so that when the subject comes out of the suspended state he finds himself in another age."

"Have you any means of controlling this travel through time?" I asked.

"Not accurately," the Professor replied. "I can send time speeding on, but cannot stop them exactly on a certain day. I can stop them within a few years of my instrument, but they are not at that stage where I can send him to say— the year two thousand—and he will stop within a year or so of that."

"You can bring him back?"

"Easily. By simply reversing the whole process."

I thought to myself that I would prefer to risk my reputation to stepping into one of those cylinders, but I did not say so. The Professor might be mad or he might be inspired. In any case he was doing me a service in giving me the right—and the exclusive rights—to chronicle the narratives of his time-travellers.

"How can you be sure that these two men will come?" I asked.

"I have sent them an invitation," the Professor said blandly.

"That will hardly be enough," I remarked.

"No?" the Professor said, raising his eyebrows. "What more should they require? It is not every day they get invited to such a house and such society as this."

"That's just the point," I said. "They are down on their luck. They may be shy and in any case they are hardly likely to possess the requisite clothes."

The Professor nodded thoughtfully. "I never thought of that. We men of science are not always very practical, I'm afraid. Then what should I do?"

"Send them two complete outfits of evening clothes and send one of your cars for them about nine o'clock. Then you will be sure of having them present and also their gratitude should help you to entice them into your cylinders."

"You are right!" said the Professor. "I will do that. I am greatly obliged."

CHAPTER TWO —A TRIP?

As they walked up the drive Harry turned to Billy.

"Take a gander at that view," he said. "These toffs certainly know how to pick the spots."

"I know how to pick the spots, too," said Billy, "if they'll let me get near the bar."

The grounds of the house ran right down to the water's edge. On the left the lights of the Bridge flung a necklace across the water, opposite were the thousands of lights of North Sydney, the green and amber street lights being thrown back prettily from the water. Neon signs flashed over there, but close to them the grounds were hung with lanterns of many colours.

The house was of three stories of an old mode, but it had been modernised with marble terraces—a new innovation to Australia—though particularly suitable to the climate. The orchestra inside was just tuning-up and the house was ablaze with lights. They reached the door and presented their cards, Harry still intent on the view and watching a ferry throw its many lights on the calm grey water while Billy licked his lips at the thought of another kind of liquid.

The butler stared at the cards, then at them.

"Just a moment," he said and hurried away.

"There you are," said Harry. "I told you they were phony."

"Think we ought to run while we still have the clothes?" Billy asked. "They might want 'em back and those cufflinks and pearl studs—"

"Ssssh!" said Harry. "Don't wake up the world."

"Perhaps they want me to sing!" Billy murmured.

"And start a riot?" asked Harry. "God forbid! Let's talk about something else. Did you read that book I lent you?"

"Nearly," replied Billy. ."I have only the first few chapters to read to finish it. It's a bit highbrow for me. Those highbrow writers annoy me. They write about what they don't understand and make you think it's your fault."

An old gentleman came to the door.

"Sssh!" said Harry. "Here comes Whiskers. We should be able to handle him."

"Good evening, gentlemen," said the old man. "I am very pleased you accepted my invitation. I am Professor Slagoscar."

"How do you do?" said Harry, bowing.

"Well, well, well," said Billy. "When did we meet before?"

"Never, I imagine," said the Professor, with dignity.

"No—that's right," said Billy. "It must have been some other geezer with whiskers. Where's the bar?"

Harry kicked out at Billy and missed and the Professor stared. Then he turned and led them along a wide hall and into a large study. I was sitting there.

"Allow me to introduce you, gentlemen, to Paul de Wreder," the Professor said. "This is Henry Nash."

"How do you do?" said Harry.

He was tall, with brown hair and clear blue eyes. He carried his clothes well, was slim but seemed strong.

"And this is William Stewart."

I looked at Billy. He was very dark, brown-eyed, short and thick-set. He came up and shook hands.

"Billy to you, pal," he said, and added in a whisper, "Where's the bar?"

I winked and he grinned.

"Sit down, gentlemen," the Professor was saying. "Would you care for a drink of something?"

"No," said Billy. "Just give me a drink of everything."

"My friend," Harry said, smiling wryly, "is a great one for jokes. I'll take a pint myself—beer, with the froth on the bottom."

"I suppose you are wondering why I invited you here," the Professor said, after ringing a bell.

"I have been, rather," Harry said.

The Professor passed on our various orders to a butler who appeared.

"The fact of the matter is," said the Professor, "I think we have neglected our brave warriors. Have you any relations?"

"I'm an orphan myself," said Billy. "Except for my mother. And then there's my father, of course, but no one takes any notice of the old man."

"Where are they?" Slagoscar asked him.

"I don't rightly know," Billy said slowly. "You see they're dead."

"But you just said—" The Professor gave it up.

The drinks arrived and Harry and Billy speedily disposed of theirs. The Professor pushed forward a basin of nuts, biscuits and lollies.

"What time is your experiment timed for?" I asked.

"Have some sweets?"

"No, thanks," said Billy. "I used to have a sweet tooth, but I had it pulled out. It turned sour on me."

"What time is your experiment timed for?" I asked.

"At ten o'clock," Slagoscar replied. "It should be completed by daylight—a few minutes in each period of time should suffice."

I saw Harry staring at us. "Experiment?" he asked. "I thought you were having a reception here to-night."

"That is correct," the Professor said. "Early in the morning we will be welcoming back some time-travellers."

"Time-travellers?" said Billy. "What's that—a bunch of alarm-clock salesmen?"

The Professor smiled slyly. "Not exactly," he said. "It is a surprise. You will discover later."

"Goody," said Billy. "One of those games like 'find the thimble.' I got a prize at one of those once. It was a silver thimble and I found it first. The others are still looking."

"Now make yourselves at home," said the Professor. "I will show you the ballroom."

"Never mind about that," said Billy. "Just lead me to the bar and place a brass rail under my foot. I'll be right."

By ten o'clock he was more than right. I went to find him in the bar and discovered him behind it, serving half a dozen society beauties with fancy drinks of his own mixing.

"What are you doing?" I asked.

"Playing Aunt Sally," he said, somewhat thickly. "These drinks of mine are dynamite. You watch me knock these dames over one at a time."

"The Professor wants you in the ballroom," I said.

"What's on?" he asked.

"The time for the experiment has arrived," I said.

A gong sounded through the house and I helped Billy into the huge ballroom, followed by the ladies and everyone who was not there already.

The Professor was standing on a platform at one end, Harry beside him, and behind him were two huge glass cylinders, many tubes, glass retorts and peculiarly shaped scientific gadgets, electric wires, observation dials and levers. I half-led, half-dragged Billy to the platform. Harry was not drunk—but neither was he sober.

"He's drunk," I whispered to the Professor, indicating Billy.

"It does not matter," he whispered back. "The experience will sober him."

It should, I thought.

"Ladies and gentlemen," the Professor said, and everyone fell silent. "You are now about to see an experiment without precedent in the history of mankind. These two gentlemen are about to assist you to see into the future."

Billy was grinning widely. "Fortune telling," he giggled to me. "I'm a dab at this."

"First of all I will ask my assistants to have a drink," the Professor went on.

"He's a mind-reader," said Billy, holding out his hand.

The Professor picked up two glasses from a table. They held a small concoction of coloured liquid. He held them in his hand for a moment.

"These are a—er—cocktail of my own invention," he said. "Drink them up."

He handed a glass each to the men.

"What's wrong with it?" asked Harry.

"Nothing—nothing!" said the Professor, watching him feverishly. "Just drink it."

Harry placed the glass to his lips and then lowered it again.

"I heard a funny yarn on the bus," he said. "A feller said that half the lies told about him were not true. That was funny. But—"

"Please drink," the Professor pleaded.

Harry stared at him. "I'm going to," he said. "What's eating you?"

"Nothing. Be a good fellow and drink it up."

"Hey, wait a minute," Billy said, staring suspiciously at his drink. "This isn't the pill that will or anything, is it?"

"No—no," said the Professor, nearly frantic. "It's quite all right."

"I know a funny story, too," said Billy musingly. "A feller said that he had been to a great party. It was such a good party that he was not thirsty for two days after it. Now, I know another—"

"You can tell me that one when you come back," grated the Professor.

"When I come back?" said Billy. "But I'm not going anywhere."

"I mean, you can tell me when you've had your drink."

"I know one," chimed in Harry. "Do you know how to make razor blades last twice as long?"

"I know," said Billy "Buy your wife a pencil sharpener."

"You've heard it—"

"Will you drink those drinks?" the Professor shouted. "I'll go raving mad in a moment."

"All right—don't get excited," said Billy. "Here's the froth off your whiskers."

They drank together, licked their lips and the professor took the glasses from their hands. Then an expression or amazement came over their faces.

Suddenly they stiffened but before they could topple over they were caught by butlers who had been standing ready.

CHAPTER THREE —OUT FOR A CENTURY

The two men were placed inside the cylinders and strapped into an upright position. On their faces was a frozen expression of amazement. The Professor turned a switch and the sealed cylinders began to glow with varied coloured lights. He turned to the watching crowd.

"The experiment has begun," he said with excited satisfaction. "You have often wondered what the future holds for us and for those who come after us. These men will be able to tell us in a few hours. I have conquered the fourth dimension—Time. These subjects of' mine will shortly vanish into the mists of the future—seeing history which is as yet unmade—until I bring them back. As they go on they will not leave this spot, but to them the tubes will have vanished—and so will we. We will mostly be dead, because their first stop will be about the year two thousand. But they will be in the same situation—but how changed this room may be."

He stepped to his many levers and began to manipulate them. The cylinders glowed brighter and brighter until the glare hid the men from view. Suddenly, a switch clicked, the buzz and racket of the many instruments eased and the glow died down.

The tubes were empty!

"They have gone—into the future!" exulted the Professor. "Now I will project them forward about one hundred years."

He dropped on a stool and turned a knob, which operated an arm like that on a resistance from one terminal to another. As it leapt across sparks burst up for an instant in the cylinders—then all was still.

* * *

Billy shook his head. It ached. It felt as though he had just come out of a jag. But the ache departed speedily. Great stuff, that of the Professor's, he thought. It certainly sobers one up quickly—and leaves no ill effects.

He opened his eyes—expecting to see the sea of faces beneath him and the brightly—lit ballroom. He closed them again—swiftly. That stuff of the Professor's couldn't be so good after all. He was seeing things. He tried one eye again—and then stared.

He was in a room. It was a fairly small room and bore no resemblance to the ballroom whatever. Everything in the room was of a circular design—the furnishings, the wall, the floor, the carpet, and in the centre was a large round object with a flat top. It might have been a radio set of a peculiar design for it had knobs on the side, but the top was of ground or opal glass and was of about three feet in circumference. He guessed it might be a table.

But how did he get here? He continued his gaze and became aware that there was a man in the room. But was he a man? On a round couch was seated a person in short mauve trousers, rolled socks of the same hue, an open lilac shirt, a short black bolero while beside him was a tall hat, like a witch's.

Billy tried to blink the scene away. The room was lit by electricity and refused to be blinked away. The person on the couch was staring at him.

"Who are you and how did you get in here?" asked a man's voice.

"You're asking me!" said Billy. He looked around startled. "Where's Harry—I've lost Harry. We've become separated. He'll be useless without me."

"What in—what are you talking about?" the man asked, rising.

"My cobber—my buddy—my pal!" said Billy in an anguished voice.

"You talk strangely," the man said. "You use old-fashioned terms."

"Where am I?"

"This is my flat at Darling Point," the man replied. "Though how you got in here, I don't know."

Billy saw a window, ran to it and pulled aside the curtains. Outside was the night, the harbor and North Sydney—and yet, was it? Yes, there were the lights of the bridge to his left—but North Sydney never had so many lights before—nor so many flashing signs. And the ferries—they were huge things, like liners. There was no doubt about it—that last drink had been a beauty. Maybe he'd wake up soon.

"Who are you?" asked the man.

"I'm not too sure," said Billy. "Something's happened to me. I may be Snow White. My name is Billy Stewart."

"But what is your number?" asked the man curiously.

Billy stared at him. "Number," he said. "Regimental or gaol? Look here, I'm no convict. I—"

He stopped as the man burst into laughter. The man stared at him and laughed and laughed.

"Little Audrey's brother," Billy said. "What's so funny?"

"Those clothes!" giggled the man.

"I'm in a rat joint," said Billy. "I'd better get out—if I'm not one of the patients. What's wrong with my clothes?"

The man sobered up. "Oh, I see it all now," he said. "You are going to a fancy dress ball—that's why you are dressed in period costume. Like they used to wear in let me see—nineteen forty-five, I think."

"Well, what's wrong with that? This is nineteen forty-five, isn't it?"

The man stared at him. "You're mad—or drunk," he said. "You know very well this is the year two thousand and fifty."

"Eh!" yelped Billy. "I gotta get out of here—this guy's bats. Two thousand and fifty—you're mad."

"I'm not," said the man. "But you seem to be. Look, there's a calendar."

"I've been doped," said Billy slowly. "That's it—I'm doped. Where's a tap to shove my head under?"

"A tap?" queried the man. "What do you mean by a tap?"

"A water tap," Billy said, staring at him. "Don't you know what a tap is?"

"No—what is it?"

Billy breathed a sigh of relief. "Thank goodness it's not me that's mad," he said. "A tap is a thing you get water from."

"Oh, I understand," said the man. "I have one of those, but we call it—"

"I mean DRINKING water," said Billy.

"That's right," said the man. "We call it a cloud-pipe."

"A which?"

"You are terribly ignorant, aren't you? Don't know the simplest things. It is an arrangement which draws moisture from the clouds so that we can get water whenever we want it. Our scientists invented it, I believe, because there used to be droughts once and it was so much cheaper than building dams."

"It's a good idea that," said Billy. "But what am I talking about? This isn't real. I've had a smell—I mean a spell, cast over me."

"Number Twelve invented the cloud-pipe," remarked the man.

"Er—who?" asked Billy.

"Number F S Twelve. Surely you have heard or him! He is our greatest scientist."

"I'm a ratbag, all right," Billy told himself. "This must be a boob. I dunno. There must've been something queer about that drink. I didn't like that old joker from the start—there was something about the cut of his whiskers. I wonder—I wonder if I have been taken advantage of. Maybe he made me the subject of that experiment he spoke about. No wonder he was eager for us to imbibe that giggle-juice." He turned to the man. "What year did you say it was?"

"Two thousand and fifty."

"Geewhillikens!" gasped Billy. "I've grown a hundred years in a minute. I should be dead—but I don't smell much."

"Is there anything the matter with you?" the man asked, staring at him.

"And I've lost my cobber," said Billy. "He must have got off at the next stop."

"I think you ought to go to your fancy dress ball before you're TOO drunk," the man remarked.

"I have no ball to go to," Billy groaned.

"Well, you look very funny getting about like that."

"I can't help looking funny—it's natural. Don't you have names now?"

"No. Number A One, the great world dictator of nineteen eighty-seven, cut them out, giving us numbers instead. Names were too individualistic. So he called himself A One and so on. One must not think any more—because that is too individualistic, too."

"I never did do much thinking," said Billy. "Very few people do. Those few do the thinking and the rest believe what they tell 'em, which is mostly wrong. Well, I suppose I will have to make the best of it. I'm here and that old Whiskers would be well dead by now. My number is Umpteen."

"Umpteen?" said the man. "I've never heard of that number."

"It's an old one. You haven't heard all the numbers, have you?"

"Of course not. One could hardly hear all the numbers in a city with four million people."

"What's that?" asked Billy. "How many?"

"The population of Sydney is over four million. Surely you knew that?"

"No——I come from the country," said Billy,

"But there are plenty of cities of a million in the country. Surely they teach you things there?"

"Not much," said Billy. "Tell me, what area does the city cover now?"

"We are not in it now. It runs to about what used to be called Double Bay out this way, cuts across to Bondi Junction, in the south goes to Botany Bay and the west to Strathfield. But it is overcrowded."

"It certainly has grown some," Billy agreed. "How came that about?"

"Oh, the various wars in Europe drove people out here."

"What wars?" asked Billy.

"All the wars," the man said, staring. "We have had a war about every twenty-five years since the nineteenth century. I'm pretty good at history, but I can't remember back past the Boer War in 1900. Then there was that piffling little thing they called the World War in 1914. Then the Second World War in 1939—"

"I remember that," said Billy thoughtfully.

"Don't be ridiculous!" scoffed the man. "Although we have increased the span of life to one hundred and fifteen you could not have been born then, because you are no more than forty. Then there was the Real World War in 1965 which lasted till '87 and left Number One dictator of the world. Then came the Revolutionary War of two thousand and one, which left a new dictator and then, in two thousand and thirty, Australia rose against the world in the second Revolutionary War and left the present Number One C. The Australian, you know."

"I didn't." Billy said, wandering to the window and staring upwards, wondering if the stars were still in their places. If they were they were on the move, because everywhere he looked were lights—large and small, some short, some elongated.

CHAPTER FOUR — FRESH FACES

"What are all the moving lights?" he asked. "Fire-
works?"

The man came to his side. "Oh, those," he said.
"That is the nuisance of living near an **air-road**—the
buses and **trains** and private planes going along all the
time stop you from having your curtains open."

"But they make no sound!" gasped Billy.

"Of course not. Number D Fifty-seven eliminated
noise from plane engines during the war of 1965. Since
then he's eliminated noise from everything—except
indigestion."

Billy wandered back to the centre of .the room and
started to sit on the glass of the round object.

Don't sit on that," the man said. "I'm just going to
use it."

Billy's fertile imagination, which arose in his
stomach, immediately conjured up visions of a supper.
But you could not be sure. Maybe the people had given up
eating. God forbid!

"What for?" he asked cautiously.

"The time is just twenty-two fifteen," the man said. "I
am going to take a look at my wife."

"Your wife?" said Billy. "Don't tell me you still have marriage?"

"Well," said the man somewhat sadly, "officially they still have it. Not that it matters much to some people."

"It never did!"

"You see, I have a private detective trailing my wife."

"I see," said Billy. "There are some things which never go out of fashion."

"Love and passion will never die!" the man said morosely.

"Thanks very much," said Billy. "For your sake, though, I'm sorry."

"There's no need to be. I have my own lady friend. But it is a nuisance and expensive."

"I take it you don't mind the expense and the nuisance of the lady friend. What is troubling you is seeking evidence to cut you free so that you can begin all over again with another. It's the same old gag. Well, boy, count me in. How are we going to see your wife—trail her to the park or has her boy friend got the use of a city office?"

"They will be in the park."

"It's a wonder to me the parks are not all worn out long ago."

"My detective is shadowing them with his solo-gyro."

"The dirty dog!" said Billy. "What sort of a thing's that?"

"It's a one-man plane. He will hover over them silently with his lights out and observe them."

"Lucky dog·!" said Billy. "Then how do we get a look?"

"He has a radio-visor. With it he will transmit what he sees to me. He should be in position by now."

"Who, the detective or—ah, what's that?"

The man had touched a switch on the drum-like object and immediately the top lit up.

"I must tune in," said the man. "You can watch the top. You can serve as a witness."

"Anything to oblige," said Billy, in a voice as low as his debased morals. "Let her go—or something."

Vague scenes flitted across the glass screen and swift passing noises came from a hidden speaker—a singer—a ballet—a street—cowboys chasing an Indian—some nude studies. (Billy would have liked to see more of these but he decided they would keep—they looked healthy enough), some foreign city—scenery—a man telling the news, someone talking about nothing in superlatives—a park. The park brightened and became clearer. There was no sound, but he could see two objects moving.

"Yes," said the man. "Those are they. You can talk out loudly—they can't hear us. Ssssh!"

"Twenty-one speaking," a voice said softly from the speaker. "Am hovering over Rushcutters Bay Park. She has met B Ninety-three. I will keep high until there is more to see. You can see them looking for a spot below."

Billy chuckled. "They pick on a pretty lighted spot, don't they?" he asked.

"Oh, no. The visor sees just as clearly in the dark as in the light. It is a very sensitive instrument and then we amplify it."

He fixed his eye on the glowing glass. The pair were getting larger as the plane crept lower. He could see the woman closely now. She was a blonde and very beautiful.

For several minutes there was silence while they watched.

"Oh, this is terrible!" the man moaned. "I cannot look any longer."

He turned a switch and the glass went blank. Billy stared at it, even more blankly, for a moment, then he came to life.

"Hoy!" he said. "Don't be mean."

"I could not stand and look on at her shame any longer."

"Maybe you couldn't—but I can. Where's that switch?"

He hunted round and pressed a switch. Immediately the scene of a map in spectacles leapt upon the glass. He was pointing to a graph.

"The average population of youth in Bundaberg—" he said, and Billy turned a switch, cutting him off short in his youth.

"Come and fix this thing," he shouted to the man, dancing around in his excitement.

The man had thrown himself on the couch. "How could she be so cruel?" he said musingly.

"Cruel!" yelped Billy. "It's you that's cruel. You work a man up in suspenders like that and then cut 'em off, letting everything fall. Bah, you make me sick."

The man was not listening. "She was always like that," he said. "Fell in love with every fresh face she saw."

"I'll dash out and freshen mine up a bit," Billy remarked. "When is she due home?"

CHAPTER FIVE —PASSING THE TIME AWAY

The man rose purposefully to his feet. "When she does come home," he said, viciously tugging open a drawer and pulling out what looked like a small sub-machine gun, "I'll give her this."

"Put that away—if it's what I think it is," said Billy, "It spits. If you must give it to her make it handle first."

There was a flurry before Billy's eyes, and by the time he could see straight again, there was a girl in the man's arms.

"Darling," she said to the man. "Is wifie out?"

"Yes, saccharine—my owny own," the man burbled.

"Who's this?" asked Billy. "Is this the little flutter? She certainly moves fast."

"We waste no time these days," the man said.

Billy glanced at the glass screen. "I noticed that," he remarked. "Introduce me."

"This is my girl-friend—S Twenty-eight," the man said reluctantly. Billy and the girl looked each other over, found each other palatable and smiled.

"How's everything, my dear?" Billy said, edging closer. "How's your father? Still chasing the two-legged cats?"

"No. Ha hasn't been so well since his hundred and thirtieth birthday."

"Hey!" said Billy, and just remembered in time that it was not polite to ask a woman her age.

Then something else happened. The door opened and he turned to see a woman standing there—the same beautiful woman he had seen on the glass-screen. They certainly travelled fast, these people! Maybe she had come straight home in her rocket-ship or something. He never discovered.

"What's the meaning of this?" she asked, staring at the man with the girl in his arms. "What are you doing with that hussy?"

Billy looked up at the ceiling and began to whistle softly "The Last Post". For a moment there was silence, then the man rushed into speech.

"She is—er—she is my good friend Umpteen's wife and she has just hurt her ankle. I caught her just in time."

"Too right you did!" said Billy, as the man put the girl from him and she limped to the televisor.

"Who is Umpteen?" snapped the wife.

"Oh, I forgot," the man said, straightening his bolero. "This is Umpteen—a very distant relation of mine. This is my wife."

Billy bowed, noticing that the clothes of that period were very becoming and very revealing. The woman wore high boots with tassels at the top, a short skirt half way to her knees, and a velvet blouse with transparent inlays.

"I am one of your husband's ancestors," he remarked. "Jolly pleased to meet you."

"What a wonderful man!" she breathed softly.

"Thank goodness I have a fresh face!" said Billy.

"I've never heard you mention Umpteen before," the wife said to her husband. "You should have."

"I am secret service," hissed Billy. "I am in disguise. That's why I wear these clothes. I am disguised as a black and white barber's pole."

Billy and the wife drew together.

"I think," said the man suddenly, seeing the movement, "that you are neglecting your wife."

"Of course," said Billy, turning and sweeping the girl into his arms. "Now, let me see—we were talking about the colour of the furniture in the wash-house or somewhere, weren't we?"

He dropped on the couch and drew the girl on to his lap. She looked into his eyes in such a way that he felt the hair on his neck rise.

"Do we need furniture?" she cooed.

"Hoy!" the man yelped, moving round like a jelly with St. Vitus dance. "There's no need for that, is there?"

"We must have furniture in the wash-house," Billy said, his breath mixing with hers and making her groggy. "Your mother must sleep somewhere. Do you mind if I nibble your ear, my sweet?"

The man grasped the girl's arm and yanked her from Billy's knee—just in time.

"I thought I heard your wife say she had an appointment?" he rasped.

"Quite likely," said Billy dreamily. "She's had lots of things."

"And as you won't be going yet," the man went on, "I'll see her to the door."

And, before Billy could stop him he whisked her out of sight through the door. Billy came out of his dream and found the wife's eyes upon him.

"This is where I put on a fresh face," he murmured.

"I'm surprised at a nice man like you having a bit of a girl like that for a wife," the wife said, edging towards him.

"She's nice for practise," Billy said.

The wife dropped on his knee and pushed back his hair. "You want a woman of experience—like me," she said.

"Experience is right," Billy said, glancing at the televisor.

"I like passion—passion—passion!"

"Not three times—please!" said Billy. "Boy, what a year this is!"

She threw her arms round him and tried to kiss him and they fell backward on the couch.

"Now, break that down!" said Billy. "I bar biting!"

She kissed him several times and then just as he was trying to get his second wind, the man came back into the room, the weapon still under his arm.

"Aha!" he grated. "I have caught you at last. Now, I have the evidence for my divorce. In my own home, too. Woman, you are not fit to live. You need disinfecting."

He aimed the gun at them and Billy pushed the woman aside and sprang up.

"Don't shoot!" he yelped. "I confess everything. I am the father of the—wow!"

A stream of liquid shot from the gun and sprayed the woman. A pungent smell of disinfectant rose in the room.

"Disinfecting—that's what you need!" said the man, then turned. "And as for you, Umpteen—heavens!"

For, where Billy had been was a blur or coloured light which slowly faded out into nothingness.

CHAPTER SIX —TIME WAITS FOR NO MAN

All Billy knew was that the whole scene faded out before his eyes and he wondered for a moment; then put it down to the potency of the woman's kisses. Boy, are they strong! he mused. I've fainted or gone blind. No, what's this?

The light was coming up again, but he seemed to be in a different place. This was like a warehouse, with piles of boxes and merchandise piled up all round him. And on one of the boxes, looking very dazed sat Harry Nash.

Billy ran across the room to him.

"Harry, you old son-of-a-gun!" he shouted. "Boy, am I glad to see you! Where have you been?"

Harry took his own head from between his hands, and stared.

"Nowhere," he said. "But wherever it was I got a nice head out of it."

"That'll pass in a moment," Billy said. "I had one like that once. I thought you'd got lost."

"I could have, for all you cared," said Harry. "Where did you go to? How did you get us in this dump?"

"I never got us here at all. It was that Professor Johnny. Remember? How's the headache?"

"Gone, thank goodness."

"I've been properly through it," said Billy. "Though it had its nice curves. I've been in the eternal triangle and been disinfected!"

"Serves you right for going into a pub called 'The Eternal Triangle.' When was that?"

"Oh, about a hundred years ago, I expect."

Harry stared at him. "You're stewed—drunk—blotto!" he said.

Billy walked towards one of the broken windows. "I wonder what year this is," he murmured.

Harry stared after him. "You ARE drunk!" he remarked positively. "It's nineteen forty-five, of course."

Billy turned from the window, where he was contemplating a harbor awakening to the dawn, with huge ships close by, at wharves which had never been there before.

"Haven't you woke up yet?" he asked curiously.

"No, I'm talking in my sleep, you mug."

"But you don't understand," Billy insisted. "This is not 1945. That Professor played the dirty on us. You remember that stuff we drank? How eager he was for us to drink it?"

"He was a bit that way, but I remember when I started to drink he grinned like the top of his head was on a hinge."

"Well, they were doped. There was biteys in 'em or something. They sent us whirling over the years—hundreds of years at a jump."

"You're mad!" said Harry and looked round through the gloom for the door.

"That's what I thought at first," Billy said, nodding. "But it's right. This is the year two thousand and something odd. Come and look."

"They were doped all right," said Harry rising wearily. "You've gone nuts. Or do you mean he poisoned us and we're dead?"

"I don't feel dead," Billy said.

"There's a funny smell round here, nevertheless," said Harry.

He looked out the window—then stared. "Where are we?" he gasped.

"Don't you recognise it?" said Billy. "This was once the Professor's ballroom. The years have changed it. Sydney grew out and swept over it. It was flats the last time I saw it. Now it's a warehouse on a wharf. See, there's North Sydney."

"With all those houses and not a tree in sight? Look at the height of the joints. This must be New York."

"It's Sydney, I tell you!" Billy shouted, jumping up and down.

"Where's the bridge?" Harry asked and Billy looked.

There was no bridge, but the skies were rapidly filling with aircraft of all kinds—small and large. Billy realised that there was no need for a bridge over the harbor now.

"I wonder where we'll lob next," he murmured. "In case we get separated I'll shake hands now. Good-bye, old pal."

Harry, sniffing suspiciously to see what he had been drinking, decided to humour him and shook hands gravely.

"Maybe we'll meet again in a thousand years or so," Billy remarked lugubriously.

"It must have been great stuff," Harry said, shaking his head with envy. "Great stuff! What a jag!"

He turned once more to the window. "There is a faint resemblance," he remarked. "But all the ships seem to have wings. They're bigger than they used to be, too, and yet they look as though they fly. What a drink that must have been! I'm seeing things now. That plane there looks like one man flying. He has a basket full of milk bottles." He stared at the various curiosities for some time, then began to wonder. "You haven't really been telling me the truth, have you? Or is this some mighty queer dream?" Over his head soared a huge plane with people standing on open decks at the side. He suddenly realised that Billy had not said anything for some time.

He turned. The room was empty.

He listened. There was no sound. It struck him that that was funny, too. All those planes outside should have made a sound. He distinctly heard a voice speaking—it seemed from across the water. He felt a creepy feeling in the region of his spine. This wasn't right. No drink could have this effect. There was something queer about all this.

He looked down at the ground below the window. It was stacked with piles of lumber and there was a strange looking object on rails which he took to be a crane.

He shook his head. Queerer and queerer! Then the whole scene began to swim and fade before his eyes. "Billy!" he shouted and heard his voice from afar off.

For a moment all was black, then the light began to grow again. Harry staggered and tried to keep his feet. Then it was light and he was leaning against the wall of a room—a very plain room with low chairs of a peculiar design—most peculiar, as they seemed designed for comfort—and very little else in the way of furniture. There was a long window in the wall reaching almost from the ceiling to the floor. He was alone in the place and he crossed to the window and looked out.

By the shadows it appeared to be morning. Before him was the harbor, just as before, but with a difference. The wharves he had seen previously were still there, but they appeared to have been long in disuse and were crumbling to pieces. The hulk of a large air-boat lay near them, waterlogged and useless. Two children, about five, entirely naked, were playing on it. The waters of the harbor were packed with large and small flying boats—one of which reminded Harry of the fantastic rocket-ships he used to see in the comic strips. Some of the houses on the other side of the harbor had been cleared away, and between the giant skyscrapers were open spaces where rested land-planes.

He poked his head out the window and took a closer view of his surroundings. The building he was in went up much higher and seemed to be a tenement, surrounded by many more of the same kind.

Harry heard a noise behind him and turned as a person entered the room, humming softly and carrying a bucket and mop.

CHAPTER SEVEN —TALKING OF WOMEN—

The person stopped humming on seeing Harry, and stared back. This person had short hair, masculine features but was dressed in a short house smock, with hairy legs and big feet protruding. He, for it appeared to be a he, wore a mob-cap over his hair. Slowly he set down the mop and square bucket, placed his finger to his lips, carefully closed the door, then tiptoed to the window and drew the curtains.

"I've landed in the Queen's Club!" Harry murmured. "What's biting you?"

"Ssssh!" the man said warningly. "Are you one of us?"

"Hey, break that down, Panse," Harry retorted. "Don't tell me I look like that. What year is this?"

The man stared at him. "What year?" he echoed, and then his brow cleared. "Oh, I see—that is the password! This is the year of Liberation—the year two thousand, two hundred and fifty."

Harry blinked. "Phew!" he whistled. "How I can travel! They always told me I was pretty fast."

"Ssssh!" hissed the man in an agony of anxiety. "She might hear you."

"Who—the missus? Don't worry about her. What of it if she does? I can handle women and I'm certainly not afraid of 'em."

The man's eyes glowed with admiration. "What a hero you are!" he burbled. "And how brave you are to venture abroad wearing women's clothes."

Harry glared. "Now, listen," he snapped. "I resent that. I'm not one of your club. It's you who are wearing women's togs."

The man sighed. "Alas, how terrible it is that we have to wear these frightful things. I hate them and occasionally when she is at business I dress up in hers. Of course I have always worn these. As you know, Women began to gain the ascendancy over Man two hundred years ago and slowly they have taken over everything. I believe we wore trousers once."

Harry gasped.

"They said it was immoral for us to wear the trousers!" the man sighed and appeared about to break into tears.

"It would be more indecent without 'em," Harry remarked.

"But they said we needed clothing adequately more than they did."

"Adequately!" snorted Harry. "As long as I can remember, women have tried to do with less than was adequate. At least we covered our chests and backs and legs."

The man nodded with a dry sob. "And, since they have begun to rule, the country has been going to ruin. Of course, it was all through those many wars—it was a good argument that Man was a trouble maker and not fit to rule. But they are worse. Oh, how I long to wear her trousers!"

"I should imagine they'd be a bit slack in the seat," Harry remarked. "And women's pants are too cool for me."

"Ours are the cool kind," the man said, shyly lifting his smock and showing a pair of silk and lace "things". "Ooooh, I hate housework. Wash dirty dishes day after day, day after day; iron her shirts week after week, week after week; clean the stains off her clothes and drudge, drudge, year after year. Ashes all over the house and always picking up her cigarette butts. How I hate scrubbing...the scrubbing-machine vibrates my nerves. Lend me your hanky, I think I'm going to cry."

The man came closer, leant on Harry's shoulder and burst into tears.

"Must be pretty terrible!" was all Harry could think to say.

Suddenly the man stopped crying.

"I must finish my work," he said. "She'll be coming home from the office shortly and she might give me a beating."

Harry got an idea. "How do you get on about babies?" he asked.

"Oh, they haven't changed THAT, thank goodness," the man said, "although the scientists talk of doing so. Families are limited by law to three children so as not to hold up the world's work."

"But families are the world's work," Harry remarked. "It used to be quite a common practice—everybody had families—though the poor were the most generous."

"You are not allowed to have a baby nowadays unless you can afford to keep it," remarked the man. "The youngsters are the lucky ones. They don't wear clothes at all until they are ten."

"Both good ideas," said Harry. "Do you marry in a church?"

The man stared. "A church?" he enquired. "Do you mean a place of religious worship? Oh, no, they marry you in a government building in hundreds, after you have passed all the mental and bodily tests. The churches you speak of must have been those huge temples I have heard about. The government decided that the cost of such edifices could be better employed feeding the poor and tending the sick. They were turned into useful institutions, and all worshipping is done in the open—in Nature's own cathedrals."

"In some ways you advance—in some you don't" Harry remarked. "Where does your wife work?"

"In London. She should be home soon, because it only takes. Twenty-five minutes in the new strato-rockets. If she finds an agent of the Male Rebels' Secret Society here she will half kill me. You ARE an agent, of course?"

Harry nodded. "I'm a male rebel," he said.

"Those tyrant women would rip you limb from limb if they found you in those clothes," the man said admiringly. "You are very brave."

"Eh!" yelped Harry, his eyes popping out. He grabbed the man by the shoulders and shook him. "Do you mean that?"

"Don't be rough with me, please!" the man said "How strong you are. Would you mind killing my wife?"

Harry stared. "Do I look like Hitler or someone?"

"How is the rebellion progressing?" the man asked eagerly. "Is it nearly time to come out in the open? What are the society's plans? Have you a message for me?"

Harry grinned and sprang up on a chair. "Ah, a message from the Male Rebels—and the past. Just stand by. Ladies and—no—no ladies. Men. We are gathered here to-night to say a few scant words about scanties. Down with Woman—bless her! We must crush them—in the good old way—to us. Why should they wear the trousers—tear them off every one of them! Why should we work and drudge and milk the baby? It is not our place to feed the children—we were never intended by Nature for such a task. There is one thing they can't take from us—our beards. We have it on them there. Let's keep it on them. Let's rub our bristles on their faces until they scream for mercy—or more. Why should we stay at home and nurse someone else's baby?"

"Hurrah!" shouted the man, losing his brassiere in his excitement.

"These women!" said Harry scornfully. "Would any man—would anything—stand for them? Let me tell you, men, that the world will go to pot under women. We are now at the pots—but in the old days they were different pots—of beer. They are making us do everything while they smoke and gossip in their clubs. Now they talk of making us have the children. I, for one, refuse to have children."

Harry paused for breath and did not see that another person had slipped quietly into the room. It was a woman, with short hair and long pants. She was smoking a cigar and wore a short coat and a large brimless felt hat. She stood listening, her brow getting lower every moment. She was quite a big woman. Harry, properly wound up, went on with his speech.

"The time has come, men, to show how you are made. Even if the weather be cold you can show your spine and let them see that we have backbone. Could they do without you? I ask you—who rocks—and fills—the cradles of the world? Answer me that and I'll say you're a liar."

The man suddenly noticed that his wife was present. He went at the knees and three shades paler.

"Ssssh!" he hissed.

"Eh?" said Harry. "Bosh! Tweedledum and fiddle sticks. There's a man in everything—everything, I tell you. Who puts the buttons on their pants to save them from disgrace? Who used to zip their zippers? I ask you that?"

Harry suddenly noticed the man's attitude and expression and he came out of his dream and glanced round the room. He saw the woman, stared at her for a moment, coughed softly and got gently down from the chair.

"Er—good morning," he said. "Do you—er—need any feather-dusters, floor polish, or—"

The woman reached out a hand and picked up the mop.

"I'll teach you to get in my trousers!" she said, between her teeth.

"No need," said Harry, smiling wryly with one eye on the mop. "I know the way." Then he pulled himself together. "It's a lie!" he blustered. "I was never in your trousers."

"It's the same thing," the woman grated, balancing the mop.

"I'm sure it's not," Harry said indignantly, glancing at the window and wondering if it was safe to leap straight through it.

"You're a rebel!" the woman snarled. "I'll teach you to wear women's clothes. You PANSY!"

She drew back her arm, took aim and tensed her muscles.

She stared.

Where Harry had been was only a coloured blur—then there was nothing!

CHAPTER EIGHT —A BUNCH OF PANSIES

Billy opened his eyes and blinked. It was bright sunlight, about midday. For a moment he stood there, thinking abstractedly that as they flew through the ages the variations of the sun were making them pass through a cycle of day. It had been night in 1945, about ten o'clock.

It had been only a little later in 2050 but in the warehouse it had been nearly dawn. Now it was midday and must be a long time afterwards.

He looked around him. The place was a ruin. The sun shone on him through what had once been a roof; now all about him were crumbling walls and piles of rubble. He passed a hand over his brow and sat down in a shady corner.

He heard voices, so he got up again and peeped through a hole in the wall. Outside was what had once been a garden, but was now nothing except tangled weeds and fallen masonry. Into this garden had come three men. They were dressed in very abbreviated shorts in bright colours, tight open-necked shirts with bell-sleeves, sandals, and they had ribbons tied round their long hair. They minced as they walked.

"Blime!" breathed Billy. "A bouquet of pansies!"

"Oh, I wish these women wouldn't pester me so much," one of them said, as they strolled around, fanning themselves. "They won't give us debs a chance. One of them wanted to take me to dinner to-night and POSITIVELY wouldn't take a refusal. I knew what SHE was after, don't worry."

"It is the same with me, dear Jimelina," said another. "I can't get a moment's peace. Nowadays things are in an awful state for us men—now that they have taken all our jobs and killed so many of us off with love and starvation."

The third man flung himself down on a heap or rubble and snarled.

"Everything is going to hell—excuse my language, dears," he growled, his deep bass fitting oddly with his clothes. "Look at this place—the result of woman's rule."

"Don't be so discontented, Regisina dear," the second one said. "They are not so bad, though some of them are awfully rough. The other night when I was crossing a park two sprang out at me and I'm sure if I hadn't screamed I would have been foully dealt with."

"Aw, you debs haven't got any guts," growled Regisina. "I know you, Tomasina. You only go across those parks in the hope you will be attacked. You're looking for an early death. I'll bet you never even reach two hundred. You like them. I hate them. They only started this new fashion because they know their figures look better than ours. It was only to ridicule us—and it's not new anyhow—nothing they do is new. It is an adaptation of the ancient Greek costume."

"Now don't get highbrow, dear," said Jimelina. "Well, what can we do?"

"Do? Why, rebel, of course."

"Oh, we couldn't do that," said Tomasina. "That's been tried—twice now—once two hundred and fifty years ago and once fifty years ago and in each case the rebellion was quashed and the ringleaders were sent to the stud-farms."

"Such places would not be necessary," Regisina said, "if women had left well enough alone and not interfered with the old custom of marriage. They wanted to make a perfect race! Bah!"

"You know very well that birth-control almost wiped out the population," Jimelina demurred. "Something had to be done. Well, they did it."

"And how!" said Tomasina ruefully.

"That's just it," said Regisina. "Once we were strong enough to rebel, but now they've sapped our strength and we are too weak to do it."

Billy thought it was time to take a part in the conversation, He stepped round the ruins and came into the garden. The three men gasped at the sight of him in his evening clothes.

"Oooh, look!" said Tomasina. "What is it?"

"It's alive!" said Jimelina. "It's a new woman dressed up funny. Maybe she's come to make love to us."

"Now lay off that business!" said Billy truculently. "I'm no woman."

"Are you a man?" Regisina said, rising eagerly.

"Want me to prove it to you?" Billy asked. "I'll go home and get my birth certificate."

Tomasina turned away. "Oh, he's one of those—a feminine man," he said.

"Now, look here, Sissy," Billy growled, "I'll hand you a slosh on the ear in a moment."

Regisina drew close to him and hissed in his ear. "Hist! Are you on our side?"

Billy looked them over. "I don't think so," he said.

"Are you sticking up for man?"

"I'll do my share. What time is it—I mean, what year is it?"

"Fancy asking what year it is!" said Jimelina. "She's mad!"

"I'll SHE you in the eye in a way you won't like!" Billy growled.

"It is the year twenty-five hundred," said Regisina.

"Gee, that's the greatest jump I've ever made. I'll soon be there at this rate."

"What we want," said Regisina, "is a strong-minded man to lead us in a rebellion."

"Why?"

"Everything is upside down. Women rule the world—they are on top and man is kept under. We are in the toils of the tyrants. We want to be freed."

"Well, you can duck off now for all I care," said Billy. "Do the women wear the same costume as you do?"

"Something similar."

"This is going to be all right here. What are the hussies doing now?"

"This is our lunch-hour. We are typists attached to the establishment of Flatface."

"So you got back to names—with an 'ina' on the end of every male name. I suppose it was necessary to distinguish which sex was which. Who is Flatface?"

"Haven't you heard of Flatface, the great scientist? She is conducting experiments so as to give animals speech and reason."

"Speech and reason!" said Billy, though he should not have been surprised at anything, after his experiences. "But then they would be equal to humans—if not better."

"That's what I say," said Regisina. "I say it is a mistake. But the Women's Council says that, as they are only transferring MEN'S brains to the animals, the animals will remain inferior to women and will be only fit to do the work of the world."

Tomasina and Jimelina had been whispering in a corner. Now they tripped forward. "Let's force her to love us," they said to Regisina and seized Billy. Billy put up a heroic struggle, but was borne to the ground.

"Oooh, I'll pull your tails in a moment, you things," he snarled, struggling fiercely. "I'll call a policeman. Police! Cops! I'm being man-handled."

"Here, what's going on here?" said a brusque feminine voice. "What have you there?"

The typists leapt up and ran into the ruins, vanishing from sight. Billy wriggled into a sitting position. Standing before him was a young girl. She had short hair, was dressed in shorts and a short blue coat with brass zippers. But she was not short of everything. On her head was a blue helmet. She was pretty and well-built. Billy regarded her with speculative admiration.

"What a place!" he breathed.

"Here you—what are you doing here?" the girl asked. "What kind of thing are you?"

Billy rose to his feet and brushed the dust from his clothes.

CHAPTER NINE —THE ETERNAL TRIANGLE

"In the first place," he said, "you can scratch off that 'thing' business. I'm a self-respecting man."

"A man!" said the girl, raising her eyebrows. "Then what are you doing out of uniform? And why are you in those peculiar clothes?"

"I'm wearing 'em," said Billy. "I'd look damn funny without 'em.”

"No doubt!" she said dryly.

"Don't be so sure," remarked Billy, "I have a very fine torso."

“Let me see this tortoise," the girl said.

“I haven't got a tortoise. I said torso. My trunk—my body."

"You know it is against the law to use foreign words," the girl said reprovingly. "There is only one language in the world—the ancient English language. Have you permission from the Women's Council to dress up like that?"

“Damn the Women's Council!" said Billy looking at her legs.

The girl staggered. "A sacrilegious traitor!" she gasped. "A rebel! I'll get a reward for him. You'll have to come along with me, my good man."

"I don't mind going along with you," Billy said, in what he imagined was a "loving" voice, "but I won't promise to be a good man. Where'll we go sweetheart?"

"I'm going to take you to the lock-up. You'll get six months for this."

"Break down that lock-up business," Billy said. "I resist. I won't go."

"I warn you—I don't want to have to use force."

"I don't need it," said Billy, "but I'm not going to the lock-up—I haven't had an invitation."

She advanced on him purposefully, but before she could seize him, he clasped her in his arms, got a firm grip as she struggled, and pressed a kiss on her lips, holding the position in spite of her wriggles. After a moment she stopped struggling and lay passive.

He swept her up in his arms and she sighed

"That was wonderful!" she said. "I've never experienced anything like that before. Do some more!"

They were interrupted by a hard, metallic voice.

"What is this!" howled the voice, and Billy felt himself yanked rudely to his feet by the collar. "Some animal murdering a police officer, eh!"

Billy twisted until he could see his captor. It was a big woman in the police uniform, though with more zippers.

She shook her hand and turned towards Billy.

But her hand was empty. Billy had passed on.

Harry opened his eyes carefully, getting ready to dodge the swing of the mop. But he was in a different room now—a far different room. It seemed to be an ultra-modern flat. He looked around for a window or door. There was none—though the air was fresh. In the centre of the room was a large double bed. It was about a foot from the floor and seemed to rest on springs instead of legs. There was no other furniture. The floor was highly polished and a few articles stood about on it, mostly deep cushions. On the walls were small knobs and Harry guessed that all mirrors, tables and drawers were built into the walls and hidden behind the panelling. There was no light visible, but the place was softly illuminated.

Standing near the foot of the bed, with their backs towards him, were a man and a woman. The man was dressed in a *crepe de chine* confection which was transparent and, by the amount it revealed, it was a nightgown. The woman was attired in short black, wide trousers, with an apron effect, the upper part of her body was covered by an article which looked like a white waistcoat and over this she wore a cape. On her head was a tall triangular hat and she carried a cane, in the handle of which seemed to be such gadgets as a cigarette-lighter, bottle opener, knife and many other things of which Harry could not tell the purpose.

Both man and woman were very well-built, big and beautiful. Neither wore make-up. The woman was pleading with the man, who stood pensively plucking at his negligee.

"Dear! Dear, won't you listen to me? Please! Please!"

The man shook his head. "I mustn't," he said sadly. "It wouldn't be fair to her. She has been kind to me—she has given me everything. Please do not tempt me."

"But love laughs at barriers—and I love you, darling I love you."

The woman seized the man and threw him down upon the bed.

"Well, well, well," said Harry, coming forward. "Excuse me. Am I intruding?"

The woman sprang to her feet. "I might have expected this," she snarled. "A private detective."

"Nothing of the sort," said Harry. "Just a traveller passing through. Carry on. I always was a devil to learn."

"What sex are you?" the woman asked.

"Well, now you're asking me something," Harry said, leaning against the wall and feeling for a bumper. "Things are a bit mixed nowadays."

"Can't you tell?"

"I never tell anything," said Harry cautiously. "That bed's a bit inconvenient, isn't it? It's so low you couldn't push anything underneath."

"We don't want to push anything—underneath."

"You two married?" Harry asked, casually, pushing the bumper into shape.

"Yes—but not to each other," the woman said. "Curse them for reintroducing marriage. I preferred the stud-farms."

"So would I," said Harry, lighting his bumper.

"I suppose you are an animal of some sort?" the woman enquired. "A baboon, perhaps?"

"I get nothing but compliments," said Harry. "If I were an animal now could I talk?"

The woman stared at him curiously. "You don't know the simplest things!"

"Maybe I do and maybe I don't," Harry said. "You go ahead and teach me."

The woman gave him a glance, then dropped on the bed and swept the man into her arms. The man gave a little squeak. Harry smoked placidly. The pair on the bed kissed. Then a portion of the wall slid back, disclosing a doorway. Harry noticed that at last the sensible scheme of sliding a door into the wall, and thus saving space, had been adopted universally. In the doorway stood another woman dressed similarly to the first woman and just as beautiful. Vaguely Harry wondered at her age. She looked at the two on the bed and her face contorted with jealousy. Some things never change, Harry thought—love, hate, jealousy, rage. Human nature has never changed in its fundamentals,—and never would.

"Aha—I have caught you at last!" said the new arrival.

Those words sound familiar to me, thought Harry, putting his foot on his bumper.

The man on the bed struggled free. "It is my wife!" he gasped.

The interloper rose to her feet. "Well, even if you have caught us," she said, "What then?"

The wife dropped off her cape. "You will take off your cape and fight like a woman!" she snarled.

I might be able to write a book on this, thought Harry, sizing up the combatants.

"Stop—stop!" squeaked the man. "Please do not do anything rash, boys. I—I am not worth it."

"I know that," said the wife, "but she has tarnished my honour!"

"I will fight you," said the interloper. "Anywhere—any time—and with any weapons."

The man sat in the centre of the bed, which danced about with every movement, squeaking and twisting his nightgown in his terror.

Hubby will tarnish his nightie in a moment, Harry thought, if he keeps twisting it about like that.

"I will fight you with bare fists, like a woman should," said the wife. "And whoever wins takes Harold."

I don't think I'll have a ticket in this sweep, Harry thought. The prize isn't worth it.

"Whatever shall I do?" the man squeaked.

"You won't have to worry," said Harry. "There's sure to be one of 'em left. I'll take the leavings."

When he spoke the wife noticed him for the first time and the others remembered him. Three pairs of eyes stared at Harry.

"What of my child?" asked the man. "My poor little child. It is not eighty yet."

"What is this thing?" the wife asked, pointing to Harry.

Harry drew himself up. He did not like the way that one spoke. He hoped the interloper won. No one answered her.

"Have it removed and thrown in the rubbish chute," the wife snapped.

"I can only stand a fair amount of this," Harry growled.

The man sprang up from the bed. "My child—I must go to my child!" he squeaked, ran to the wall, pushed aside a panel and vanished from view.

"I hope the baby is not hungry," Harry said, smiling on the rivals.

CHAPTER TEN —BUSHED

"And now," said the wife to the interloper, "You will settle up with me."

"Let her have the bed," Harry said. "She'll never get it through the door."

"It will be better if he goes with me," the interloper said proudly, having descended from a lot of proud-flesh, "I can support him and his child in greater comfort."

"His place is here," snarled the wife, "On my lowly couch."

"Lowly is right," remarked Harry, "So low you can't put a—anything under it."

"It is useless talking," went on the wife. "Let us fight for him—and may the best woman win."

"Go to it, girls," urged Harry. "I'll hold your pants—I mean, coats."

The two women threw their capes to Harry, who immediately searched for the pockets, if any. There was one pocket in each, but in neither was there anything worth souveniring.

"Rounds or to a finish?" asked the interloper.

"To a finish! Ready?"

The interloper nodded and they put up their fists in workmanlike fashion and began to circle for an opening. Neither seemed too eager to begin. The man rushed in again, nighties and all.

"Stay! Stay!" he squeaked.

"He's brought his stays with him," Harry remarked.

The women stopped circling like two angry hens, and turned to him.

"What is it, dear one?" the interloper asked.

"I have decided that you two women are too rough for me—if you fight each other you might fight me, and I could never bear that."

"You couldn't bare much more," Harry remarked.

"So I have got myself another girl-friend!" the man concluded.

"What!" yelped the wife. "Bring her in here and I'll tear her limb from limb."

The man turned in the doorway. "Come in, darling," he cooed. A large hairy ape, dressed as the women, came in, grinning broadly.

"Hello, girls," it said. "Who wants a fight?"

Harry felt his senses swimming. He decided on an experiment. He clutched the capes tight as the room spun before him—spun until it was just a blur—and then slowed down again. The scene had changed. He was standing under a large tree and before him was the harbour in the late afternoon sunlight. He blinked his eyes.

Only two huge rocket planes rocked on the water. On the other side of the harbor were only a few ruins and much parkland. In the air a few planes flashed by with almost the speed of light, though he could see a few more further up— away up, so that they must be large. They were travelling very fast.

He swept his eyes to left and right. Except for a few ruins, wherever he looked were wild trees and bushes. Sydney might have slipped back to B.C.—before Cook. One curious circumstance he noted. Dotted over the landscape were several steel domes close to the earth. They looked like huge silent cops[1], but they appeared to have windows in them and peculiar spikes jutted from them which might be some kind of guns. He brought his eyes to the nearer landscape. Everywhere was untouched Nature—trees, bushes, rocks, sand.

"Fancy meeting you again," said a voice, and he turned to see Billy leaning against a tree.

---

[1]A 'silent cop' is a raised, domed metal fixture that used to mark the centre of a side street at an intersection. It was supposed to discipline drivers so as to avoid crossing the centre-line of a street when turning. Striking a silent cop with a tyre must have knocked a car out of its path and caused its share of accidents - Editor

"Hello," he said. "That Professor must have some way of bringing us together, though he does not leave us long that way. I'm getting peckish. Struck anything to eat or drink on your travels?"

"Nary a bite—not even from a flea," Billy replied. "What have you got there?"

Harry remembered the capes. They were still in his hand. He threw one to Billy.

"Have a cape," he said. "Latest fashion of about the year twenty-seven hundred. I picked them up last stop. I suppose they think I pinched them and will have the cops out after me. A great chance they'll have of catching me. Even their fastest planes can't keep up with me."

"They live a hell of a long time nowadays," Billy said, fixing the cape. "Have you met anyone twice?"

"No, though we always seem to land in the same place, and, boy—how that changes. Everybody seems to have deserted the old city."

"Maybe a war wiped 'em out or something."

"It's a fast life," said Harry. "The last time I stopped I must have been getting on for three thousand."

"You don't look it," said Billy, "though there's a funny smell around here—"

"I don't feel it," said Harry. "I haven't had a chance to feel anything so far."

"I have," said Billy thoughtfully. "Um-hum. By the way, I met some royalty not long ago—but they weren't kings."

"What is it they call a king for short?" Harry asked.

"Rex?"

"That's it. Well, at my last stop I met Mrs. Rex—and a talking animal."

"Yeh?" said Billy, interested. "So they did that, did they?"

"Did what?" asked Harry.

"Made 'em talk. Looks like a storm working up."

Harry looked up at the sky. Dark clouds were banking up. There was a roll of thunder and a flash of lightning. The wind began to speed up.

"We shouldn't be standing under a tree," said Harry, shouting above the wind. "Some things never change. For all the civilisation and great inventions we are still children in the hands of Nature. Look how these trees have grown on the ruins of Man's edifices. We can't change Nature. Think of it—for thousands—no, MILLIONS—of years, the same old storms have raged over the earth—rain, lightning, thunder, flood. Nature unchanging—Nature everlasting."

Thunder rolled again and lightning flashed through the murk. Its brilliance showed them a crowd or objects hurrying along some distance away. They were animals, but Harry and Billy never thought of that.

"Everyone's not dead," said Harry. "I just saw a bunch of sheilahs hurrying in out of the wet—all in their fur coats."

"I wonder how they all got fur coats?" Billy asked.

"That's under the lap, I suppose."

"That's what I thought," said Billy.

Suddenly the rain descended in a rush. Billy wrapped his cape around him and crouched under the spreading branches of a tree. Lightning flashes occasionally showed him hurrying figures—all in their "fur coats". It was just a thunder-storm, but a violent one. He wondered where the people were going. He decided to ask Harry if he knew anything about it.

But when he looked there was no Harry.

Harry had leapt onward into time.

CHAPTER ELEVEN —PUTTING OFF DOG

Billy shrugged. He was getting used to this now, although he thought it rather unfeeling of Harry to leave him at this time—leave him out in the wet while he went somewhere dry.

As the rain teemed down he peered through the dim light. Not only had Harry left him, but everyone else seemed to have done the same thing. There were no more fur-coated figures—they had vanished somewhere. It was like the deserted village—only more so. Well, it was no use moaning. He would just have to wait until the Professor threw him onwards again.

Silence had fallen. No—it was not perfect silence. There was "something"—he could not place it exactly. It was a low rumbling, like machinery. But machinery had been made noiseless—though that might have been changed, of course. Somewhere, faintly, a siren whistled—there was a hiss of steam—dull explosions—crashes and rattles. Billy could not place its source.

He looked up in the air. It could not be birds—there did not appear to be a bird left. Perhaps the planes had crowded them out of the skies. In any case they would have to be very big birds to let out noises like that. He looked around him. The light was good now, but there was not a soul in sight. He noticed for the first time that the ground was vibrating. Earthquake? No, it was too regular for that.

He dropped down to the wet grass and placed his ear to the ground.

The noise was much louder now. Inside the earth there was machinery working. A sort of "Internal" machine, he thought.

A very human moan brought him to his knees, gazing about him anxiously.

"Very pleasant!" he thought.

There was a long piercing shriek.

More and more pleasant! Then out of the trees staggered a very old man with a white beard—a long white beard. It was all of four feet and almost tripped him. He was using a stick to help him along, wore a tall pointed black hat and a long black cape.

"Ah," said Billy. "Who said there was no Father Christmas? Or is it a witch?"

The old man stopped and peered at him. "Away! Away!" he croaked. "It's coming!"

"What is?" Billy asked. "Christmas?"

"No! The Chief Dog—THE CHIEF DOG!"

"A sheep dog?" asked Billy. "Where's the goats?"

"The Chief Dog, I tell you," the old man screamed. "The ruler of them all."

"That's all right," said Billy pleasantly. "I'm not afraid of dogs. There's plenty of other trees. What year is this?"

The old man stared at him. "You don't know what year it is?" he said softly, peering.

"No. What year is it?"

"It is strange you asking that," the old man said. "Many years ago, when I was only a youngster of a hundred odd, a man asked me, about this very spot—" He paused, then screamed: "You're the same man!"

"I have a habit of asking the year," Billy said, trying to place him. "On account of me not having a watch."

"Remember me—remember me?" the old man said. "I used to be a typist in Flatface's establishment. I revolted and was sent to the stud-farms. That's why I'm so old for my age. My name is Regisina."

"Well, well, well," said Billy, holding out his hand. "My old friend, Regisina. Tell me, what happened to that police dame?"

"Goodness knows! Nothing is the same now." He drew back. "You don't seem any older and you seem to be wearing the same sort of clothes."

"The same clothes," said Billy nodding. "I'm a time traveller—bewitched, you know. Again I ask—what year is it?"

"The year three thousand."

"My, my!" said Billy. "How time presses. I must hurry on—I have an appointment in the year four thousand."

"You'll never get there," said Regisina, "unless you run to your hole now."

"I can't," said Billy. "I don't possess a hole. Do you think I'm a snake or something?"

"Come, come!" snapped Regisina. "If you have no home you can come with me and I'll shelter you in my hole."

Billy put his head on one side. "That might be risky," he said. "You might be an old man but you also might be a dirty old man. Anyhow, what is this business about holes and all the silly things going on here? What is that noise like machines?"

"Those are the power machines packing away the water from the recent downpour and lighting up the city."

"But it's daylight!" Billy said.

"Not down below the surface of the earth it's not. Down there it is always night."

"Down below? Then everything must have gone to hell!"

"It has—it has!" agreed Regisina.

"You said it would," Billy ruminated. "Do the women still rule?"

"Not now—not now!"

"Ah, I see—man is on top again. I knew that would come."

"Not man—not man," croaked Regisina. "Animals rule the surface of the earth. Since they were given reason and speech they have overrun everything. You see, they do not practise birth control."

"So I've noticed," Billy remarked dryly. "We once kept a she-dog."

"They are just getting civilised. They have driven humans to earth, as the humans used to drive them to earth. At first they fought amongst themselves—the wild against the domestic. The wild won, naturally, and the domestic went over to them. But the domestic knew more about man's habits and they are the brains of the enemy. They are more vicious than the wild ones, because they remember that Man only used them for his own purposes and often treated them very cruelly—locking them out in the cold, feeding them wrongly and so so. So we built our cities under the ground, because they have the planes and bomb and machine gun us on the surface. We have secret entrances. Ah, me, I am not as young as I used to be. I will be six hundred and ten next week."

"Six hundred and ten!" gasped Billy. The old man nodded miserably. "I know you are surprised to see me looking so old for such a young age, but I have had a lot of worry. There has been no sickness for hundreds of years, but I have been unfortunate. I have had three terms at the stud farm and then, when marriage came back again, every wife I had used to leave her job and I had to go out to work to keep them and the children. Ah, for those good old days of Socialism about the time I was born."

"Don't they fight the animals?" Billy asked.

"Of course. And we kill a few, though we don't eat them any longer. It would be like cannibalism. They don't think the same—they eat us when they get a chance."

"Do many men get killed?"

"Not many men. There are not many left. They are only allowed to serve as nurses and runners. I had four proposals of marriage to-day."

"Things must be bad!" said Billy. "Maybe they want your whiskers for a rug. How do you get on for food down below?"

"We grow things, but I do miss the meat I ate in my infant days. Ah me, in another three hundred years I'm sure we'll all be dead!"

"Well, you ought to be by then, you dirty old man. What are you doing up here—trying to sheik a porcupine?"

"I am looking for strangers to lead them to the holes— the secret entrances to the city. That is my job."

Billy jumped as he heard a scream close by, and then a girl in a tattered uniform swept by at tremendous pace.

"Who threw that?" asked Billy, looking round:

The girl had vanished.

He was just taking his breath when something else flew past—another girl in uniform screaming "The Chief Dog!"

"What's this," asked Billy, "A funeral procession?"

"No—it is the Chief Dog," the old man yelled. "He is headed this way. We must get into our holes before he sniffs them out."

He hobbled away swiftly into the bushes, leaving Billy standing dazed. By the time he collected his senses the old man had vanished and Billy was alone. With what?

CHAPTER TWELVE —DOGGED BY FATE

Billy began to run round in circles. "Hoy, boy! Old 'un!" he called. "Where's my hole? I don't want to be a pomeranian's supper. I don't—" He was just thinking of climbing a tree when he stopped dead.

Through the trees leapt a huge sheep dog, which then dropped on its rump about ten feet away and regarded him, licking its lips.

"Shoo—shoo!" said Billy desperately. "Nice puppy—nice puppy. I must get you a pussy. Puss, puss—pup, pup, pup!"

"Don't talk to me like that," the dog barked. "I'm not a pansy!"

"Ooooh, it talks!" Billy groaned. "Gee, I wish I had a hole. Pretty puppy, Mummie's ikkle doggie. Does he luv his muvver?"

"You will be another one to feed my army," the dog growled calmly.

"Oh no, wait a minute. That's not fair to the army. I might poison 'em. I'll tell the R.S.P.C.A." [Royal Society for the Prevention of Cruelty to Animals –ed.]

"Bah!" the dog barked haughtily. "Don't yap back at me—I am the Chief Dog, ruler of the earth and all that's on it."

"Oh, well, I'll take to the water. Britannia still rules the waves, I hope."

The dog slapped his lips. "On second thoughts," he whined, "I think I'll eat you first and to hell with the army! Come 'ere."

"I object to that," said Billy, dancing up and down like a little boy with a reason. "Fair's fair! I don't want to eat you. Really, be reasonable!"

The dog rose slowly and stepped, half crouching, towards Billy. Billy watched it fearfully, and prepared to punch and kick. Oh, Professor, he prayed, now is the time to shove me on a million years or so.

The dog sprang, its huge red jaws extended. They closed with a snap which jarred every tooth in his head.

For Billy had vanished.

Harry kept his eyes wide open as the scene swirled like columns of smoke in a whirlwind. The colours were mostly green and as the swirl slowed to a standstill, the predominating colour was still green.

He was in a glade, but it showed signs of man's handiwork. It had many stumps of trees, sawn off neatly, and over to one side was a log hut. Through the trees he could see signs of other log huts and the grass was short, with paths worn here and there. On his left, through the trees, he could see the harbour. There were no air-boats on it now—in their place were rough canoes.

On the other side of the harbor, among the trees, were small and large log huts. Evidently Man was starting all over again.

He walked quietly across the clearing to the log hut. A window was open and he peeped in.

Seated at a table set for breakfast was a woman in a ragged dress and a large tom-cat dressed in short pants and waistcoat.

What's this? Harry wondered. An old maid and her tom-cat eating breakfast?

"Hurry, Tom, dear," the woman said to the cat, "or you'll be late for work."

Harry stared at the cat again. Surely it was not the woman's husband! It was about half the size of a man and its face resembled a man's as much as a cat's.

"Don't worry," the cat purred, "I'll beat the boss in—the old cat!"

Harry gasped. So animals still had the power of speech. He wondered what a cat could find to talk about. The cat rose to his feet, twirled his long moustache, brushed the crumbs off his vest, walked round the table and kissed his wife on the forehead.

"Good-bye, darling," he said. "I will not be home to tea—I have a lot of work to finish."

Harry watched him out of sight, then went round to the door and stepped into the house. The woman looked up sharply from clearing the dishes.

"Oh, you startled me!" she said. "I'm sorry—I can't buy anything to-day."

"I'm not a canvasser," said Harry, leaning on the edge of the door and regarding her. "I'm—I'm just a reporter."

"Reporter?" she queried. "What's that?"

"Don't you have newspapers in this year of—?"

"Thirty-five hundred. No, I have never seen a newspaper. I have read about them in history, of course. First they were on paper, then radio, then auto-printers—"

"Auto-printers?" asked Harry.

"They used to have a roll of paper in a machine," the woman explained. "As the news happened it was printed in a central office; in every home that had a machine it came over the air and was printed on the roll. Then there were the public newspapers. They were big opal screens hung in various places and on these they used to project the contents of the rolls as well as newsreels and so on. But newspapers were used so much for propaganda people stopped reading them. All that died out long ago. There were the great depressions, then the Animal Wars and so on."

"What caused these depressions?"

"They say that away back, about sixteen hundred years ago, Man ruled the earth and Woman was very jealous.

Then, through Man's foolishness, Woman slowly got a foothold and as she rose to the top she tried to crush Man in every way. Those of the men who were not turned into slaves or killed in wars took the space ships and flew off to another planet—never coming back."

"That cat," said Harry. "Was he your husband?"

"Tom?" said the woman. "Yes, he's my husband. Who did you think he was?"

"How was I to know he wasn't the boarder? Such things still go on, I suppose. Those slinky guys with moustachios! You are a woman, aren't you?"

"Yes, aren't you?"

Harry sighed. "How long is this going on?" he groaned. "I'll travel in the nude—then they can't get mixed up. Why don't you marry a man?"

"They are too scarce. Only the very rich can get men. They are very valuable and if you own a man you can let him out and make a lot of money. Of course, they don't last long."

"I'm going to like this place," Harry remarked.

"We are only allowed to have one husband a year—of any kind. The trouble is that the women have become so physically strong that nearly all the children are females."

"I can see there is work for me here."

"So this year I had to marry Tom."

"Living a sort of cat and dog life," said Harry. "Can't something be done about more males being born?"

"Like the termites, you mean? Bringing forth whichever sex they please? They have tried every means they could—chemicals, synthetic children and so on—but it still happens that most of the births are females. One of our scientists is working on an idea now. She is trying to perfect a mechanical man to serve the purpose."

"Good heavens! I'll have to carry a tin-opener."

"The robot's limbs will be of metal," the woman went on, "'but inside will be a mechanical nerve system and a brain. There is a great deal of talk about it and it is likely to work. The robots can be made so strong that maybe the sexes will be levelled."

Harry shook his head. "It's too deep for me," he said. "How can they—but, let it pass. You don't look too prosperous."

"It is the Great Depression which followed the last Animal War. Now we are at peace and trying to get the world going again. I lived most of my early life underground. It is really the politicians who are to blame for everything."

"So I've heard before," said Harry.

"Now you must excuse me while I get my kiddies off to school." She called into an inner room. "Time for school, dears."

Harry was pleased when the scene began to swirl before his eyes.

85

CHAPTER THIRTEEN —OILED!

Billy had closed his eyes tight when the dog leapt at him and he kept them closed waiting for something to bite him. But nothing happened, so he carefully opened one eye—then the other.

He was in a different place! That was good—anywhere was good, so long as it was away from that dog. He was standing in a garden—if you could call it a garden.

A road had been built in the old spot and a large building constructed. It was a long, low building like a factory, with opaque glass walls and roof. From within came the sound of machines and the clank of tinware.

It was daylight. He stepped back to get a better view. Along the side of the building was a sign "Brass and Company - Robot Manufacturers." "You always can—with a B-Co. Man." "Our mechanical men go further in the long run. Ball-bearing."

Billy looked over at the harbor. There was a wharf nearby with a large air-boat tied up. Into it boxes and cases were being loaded by some shiny objects which appeared to be men, but were too far away to be very distinct. Out on the harbor were other airboats and, on the north shore, log huts and more elaborate houses could be seen among the trees. There was no sign of the bustling activity of the air age—no skyscrapers—and not so many planes in the air. But it was a slight improvement on the last time he had seen it. He heard a clank nearby and he turned—and gasped. Coming along the street was what appeared to be a man, but was not a man. It was built in the semblance of a man and about the size, but it was made entirely of metal. It staggered stiffly as it walked—like a tin toy representing a drunken man. Across its chest was painted a number, like the registration plate of a car in the old days,

The robot staggered along the footpath, taking no notice of Billy. Billy gulped.

"Something queer here," Billy murmured, and followed the robot.

The tin-man led him down the street to near the corner of the building and then turned across the garden and went through a door. When Billy came to the door he saw a sign on it—"Dr. Steel, M.D. (Mechanical Doctor). Specialist in robot innards and illnesses of the mechanical man. B-Co Men at reduced rates."

Billy walked through the door and found himself in a long room. At the end nearest him were several forms on which were seated three robots, evidently waiting. At the other end was a cross between a doctor's surgery and an engineer's shop.

There were several objects which looked like sterilisers, one of which was marked "De-ruster", there was a chair and an operating table. Along the back was a long bench on which rested nickelled hack-saws, footprints, wrenches, spanners, engineer's hammers, and such tools. To the left was a lathe and, to the right, a forge and crucible. There was also an emery wheel and a small circular saw.

A doctor and nurse stood there, attending to a patient. They appeared to be both women. Two wires were attached to the robot who was emitting electric sparks from his mouth.

Billy glanced round at those waiting. One appeared to be a woman robot. She was staring, with eyes which glowed with an inside light, at Billy. He slid onto a seat unobtrusively. Another robot was huddled in a corner looking very miserable and not taking notice of anything. The third and last one was the drunk, who wobbled about on his seat.

All wore number plates and Billy thought what a good idea it was to have eyes which shone; they could see in the dark.

He looked back at the doctor who had removed the wires; and the sparks had stopped. She slapped the robot on the back. There was a loud hollow "Dong!"

"That fixes you," said the doctor. "Come back and see me next week, so that I can have another look at your re-charger. Good-bye. Pay the nurse at the desk."

She looked up the room, opened her mouth to say "Next please," but just at that moment the drunk slipped off his seat with a noise like a tin-shanty collapsing. The doctor walked purposefully up the hall and stood over the drunk.

"Drunk again!" she said with disgust. "You are always getting oiled. How many gallons of oil are you drinking a day?"

The robot looked up from the floor. One eye was out and the other flickered like a dying Neon sign.

"Ten!" he said greasily.

"I told you you must not exceed two," the doctor thundered. The robot put up his hand and turned his nose upside down in a peculiarly insulting way.

"So did four other doctors," he said metallically.

The doctor bent down and jerked him to his feet. It did not require much effort, so Billy deduced they must have invented a new lightweight steel or aluminium.

"Let me examine you," the doctor said, giving the robot a tap on the chest with a hammer.

Immediately there was a loud crash inside the robot's chest.

"Ah!" said the doctor. "That's the trouble with being too tight. I'll have to loosen your nuts."

"Not too loose doctor," the drunk said, thickly, as though afflicted with repeating axle-grease. "The last time you loosened them, a bolt fell off."

The doctor placed a stethoscope to the robot's chest. "Umm," she said, after a moment, "You're missing on a cylinder or two."

"My main trouble," said the robot, "is my arm. It seemsh to have losh all sensation."

"Let me have a look at it," the doctor said, giving the arm a rap with her hammer, at which there was a cracked sound. The doctor took the arm in her hands, made an adjustment near the shoulder, gave the arm a twist and it came off loose. Billy stared at the robot, but he did not seem to be affected.

The doctor took the arm down to the bench and examined it, giving it little taps with her hammer. The robot teetered on his heels while he waited. The doctor came back without the arm.

"I'm afraid you'll have to leave that arm for a few days," she remarked.

"Bud I can't do thash," the drunk said, spraying oil on the doctor. "Thash the hand I eat and drink with. Thash my right hand."

"That's what I thought," said the doctor. "If that's the one you drink with, you'll be better without it for a few days. Use the other hand."

"But I can't eat with thash one—thash the one I—"

"Sorry, but owing to a rush of orders I can't have your arm finished before Wednesday. You've worn out one of the fingers and the elbow."

"Thish terrible," the drunk mumbled. "I mush have thash hand—I'm jush married."

The robot staggered out and the doctor turned and looked at Billy.

Billy wondered if she was considering what part of him to unscrew.

CHAPTER FOURTEEN —A NEW TINTYPE

"Next please," she said.

With a loud clang the third robot slipped off the seat and lay still.

"Quick, nurse," said the doctor. "Bring some petrol—patient has konked out."

The nurse ran up with some petrol and a funnel. They lay the robot on its back, put the funnel down its mouth and poured in the petrol, measuring the amount by a dial on the wrist of the robot.

"Seems to be starving," said the nurse sympathetically.

"Yes—malnutrition of the valves. Better give him some oil, too. He seems to have plenty of water."

When the robot had absorbed about four gallons of petrol and a large quantity of oil—applied through the nose turned upside down—it still lay supine. The doctor opened a door in the side and found the battery was flat.

"Very run down," she said. "In the last extremities. Poverty, I suppose."

"But how could that be?" the nurse asked. "The robots are not free-agents. This one must belong to someone."

"That someone may get into trouble over this," said the doctor ominously. "She should not own a robot if she cannot afford to feed it and keep it in condition. Look at this poor devil. He hasn't been decarbonised since heaven knows when, and he's all rusty in places. His fingers are worked to the inner-rods. Yes, I can see someone getting into trouble over this. Get the starter."

The nurse brought two wires and attached them to terminals in the robot. Then she swung a lever, there were sparks, the robot spluttered and the eyes leapt into light again.

"How do you feel now?" said the doctor kindly.

The robot's eyes glowed. "I feel very good—well, as well as can be expected."

"What did you come to see me about?"

"I'm falling to pieces," said the robot miserably. "Last night I lost the ball-bearings off my big end!"

The doctor helped him to his feet and passed him to the nurse.

"Fix him up, nurse," she said. "Doesn't matter about the bill." Then she turned to Billy, "What do you require?"

"Me? I—er—you see, I—er—well—er—yes, that's right," Billy spluttered.

"If you were a robot with that mis-fire I'd give you a dose of oil," the doctor said. "But as you are not, perhaps you will tell me what you're here for. Did you call for an order?"

"No. I wanted to buy some—er—rabbits—er—robots. Yes; nice, fat, greasy robots with chromium platings and—er—gadgets."

"You have come to the wrong place," the doctor said. "This is the repair department." She walked down the room. "Nurse, when you have attended to that patient take that woman to the sales department."

Billy looked round for the woman and then realised that they meant him. He let it pass—which was maybe just as well for his health. He sat there waiting, hoping that he would vanish into thin air and appear somewhere else. But he did not, and soon the nurse came and led him through a door and down a passage to a large department.

It was like a store. Everywhere stood robots, large, small and medium. All glowed with the lustre of the new chromium. They were still and the lights in their eyes were out. In glass cases were various shining parts displayed. Some of the faces were quite pretty, though stiff, and the long coat effect had hinges and flaps and doors on it.

Two robot saleswomen were strolling about and one came towards Billy.

"This lady requires a robot," the nurse said and departed.

"Oh, yes," the robot said. "What type do you prefer? Is it for a husband or work purposes?"

"Er—yes. Eh?"

"The husbands are far more expensive, of course," the robot went on. "They have to undergo clinical treatment and be serviced periodically."

"I wanted a few—er—sort of servants," Billy said. "Female."

"I see. We have them only in three sizes now, since the standardisation of parts came in. Perhaps you would like to see some?"

Billy nodded and the robot led him across the room to several of the latest models.

"Now this one," she said, "is particularly adapted for washing clothes. You will note the long-tapering fingers for wringing and the strong mechanism of the wrists. She does seventy to the gallon, has all forward gears and reverse, with a special silent gear-change, has great accessibility and smooth-running. Feet are shod with non-slip rubber and if you want to marry her off at any time we supply the necessary extra parts."

"Thank you," Billy gasped. "I don't feel very well. I think I will come in again."

"Very good," said the robot. "Sorry. This way out."

She pushed Billy down in a chair, which immediately began to move and carried him swiftly, until he found himself on the footpath. The chair hesitated there, evidently for him to alight, but he was too slow, and suddenly the chair vanished into the ground and he found himself sitting in the dust.

"Some escalator!" he remarked, and then turned to see what a loud clanging din was about. Three robots, who wore strange hats like policemen's helmets, were dragging a fourth one along towards the doctor's door.

Billy stepped aside for them to pass.

"What's wrong?" he asked. "Has his fly-wheel run amok and sent him mad?"

The big robot in the hands of the others struggled and ground his gears.

"No," he snarled. "I'm a wharf-labourer-robot and I led this week's strike. We want more nuts. I know what they are going to do. They're taking me along to the doctor to have my arms taken off or my voice-box extracted. I won't stand for it—there'll be others after me. We are not getting fair treatment from the humans. Slaves, that's all we are. You'll see, one of these days these fools will wake up to themselves and then we'll see what chance the humans have! We'll show 'em. We are superior in every way. Let us be trained as mechanics and we'll be in control, because we can attend to each other. They won't allow that, but we are learning secretly. We'll show 'em—we'll show 'em."

Still raving, he vanished into the doctor's door. Billy allowed his breath to escape, leaned against the wall and slowly faded away.

CHAPTER FIFTEEN —UNDER THE STA(I)RS

Harry heard the bomb explode before he opened his eyes. He knew the sound of a bomb-burst well. He opened his eyes and looked upward at the stars.

A wall was toppling towards him. Like lightning he dashed across the street and into an open door; wondering what he had stumbled into this time.

A woman, dressed in shorts and a tight sweater—which was how he knew she was a woman—was crouched just inside the doorway. She grabbed him by the arm.

"This way," she said, and rushed him inside, along a hall and into a cupboard under the stairs. They both crouched there together.

"What's on?" Harry asked, breathlessly.

"High explosive!" the girl replied.

"I know that," said Harry. "But—you see, I only arrived in town to-day. Who's fighting now?"

"The same old robots," said the girl. "They've been doing it for ten years now—since the year thirty-seven hundred. But we'll beat them yet. We're getting control of the petrol."

"How are you off for men?"

"We practically haven't any. The robot idea never worked out and we couldn't even get any synthetic men. We have a few, of course—those who arrive naturally. But we have to keep those in hide-outs. They are too precious to risk. We don't want humanity to die out altogether."

"Perhaps I could do my little bit in this war," Harry mused.

"What do you mean?" the girl asked.

Before he could reply there came that most terrifying of sounds—the screech a bomb makes in falling through the air, because when you can hear that sound you know you are "for it."

Harry took a deep breath, grabbed the girl in his arms and threw her down, shielding her with his body.

They heard the bomb come tearing through the roof of the house—there was a dull thud near them—then silence. They waited

After a minute Harry relaxed.

"Must have been a dud," he said.

The girl was warm in his arms. She had not moved.

"Are you a man?" she asked softly.

"What makes you think that?" he asked.

"If you are a woman, you are a very unusual one," she said. "No woman would try to protect another strange woman's body with her own. No man would, either—although we read in historical novels that men did those things once. Why did you do it?"

"I don't know," said Harry. "Men do that sort of thing naturally."

"You ARE a man!" she said.

"That's right," he said.

"How did you escape?"

"Escape? Where from?"

"All the men are locked up in cages on the stud-farms underground," she said. "Anyhow—YOU are here now. I have never been so close to a man before. I'll never let you go."

The raid went on. A bomb burst quite close to them and splinters of stone and timber rained down. But they did not hear it. Harry thought: if that Professor has any decency at all he will know this is not the time to send me onwards. I'm doing all right.

Fire leapt up not far away. Another bomb burst…

When Harry managed to disentangle himself from the girl's embrace the raid had passed on and all was quiet. He could hear the girl's heavy breathing plainly.

"It gives one a very contented feeling to know that one has done one's bit in the war," he remarked.

"It does!" murmured the girl.

"Tell me about the war," said Harry, reaching out and pulling her into a sitting position beside him.

She snuggled close. "There is not much to tell," she said quite happily. "The robots rebelled ten years ago. They had been stealing secrets and training their own members as mechanics and engineers. A crowd of them got together and seized a petrol store and a factory known as B-Co. It is just across the road and I was on my way to blow it up, when our planes finished it. It looks as though my job is done, for the factory is burning. You see, when they captured the factory their engineers got to work and started turning out an army. Luckily for us they lacked the scientific knowledge to give their robots reasoning brains, but, even as mere automatons, they were terrible. Then they tried to sweep over the country capturing petrol dumps, for, without petrol, oil, and acids for their batteries, they stop after a short while. Our job was to forestall them—blow up the dumps, destroy the acids and so forth. For a while they swept over everything, because we were not prepared for war."

"One never is—till almost too late," remarked Harry,

"Their aim was to kill all humans except scientists; they took them prisoners, because of their knowledge. They captured this island, but bands of us guerrillas have been systematically blowing up the factories and dumps—by ground-work or plane. If we win, the day of the robot is done—no others will ever be made and those that do exist will be melted down. They have become too great. Those that we made ourselves, to do our work, numbered millions and our scientists gave them just sufficient sense to do the job they were made for. But their brains improved as they worked—we had not taken that into account—and this is the result."

The heat was becoming unbearable from the fire nearby. Also part of the building in which they were sheltering was burning.

"We'd better get out of here before we start to fry," said Harry, trying to rise.

The girl pulled him down again. "Not yet," she said. "Can't we—"

"No," said Harry definitely. "Not here. Come on."

He dragged her to her feet and they made for the door.

"If we meet one of these robots," he said, "how do you attack them? Bullets would not hurt tin or steel."

"They are made from a metal called oxominium," the girl replied. "It is very hard and light, but we have made bullets to pierce it. A bullet in their insides affects them much as it affects us—it destroys some organisms and puts them out of action. Here, take my spare gun."

Harry took the thing she pushed into his hand. It was shaped like a T-square—the long side being the barrel, one end of the T the grip and the other end of the T the magazine. It had no trigger.

"How do you shoot this?" he yelled above the roar or the flames, handling the gun gingerly.

"Just squeeze the grip," she said, then screamed, "Look out!"

Silhouetted in the doorway against a background of flame was a huge robot!

CHAPTER SIXTEEN —TURNING ON THE HEAT

From the robot's eyes shone two beams of light. They turned their way and the robot came stiffly forward, a huge axe in its hand.

Harry squeezed the weapon and felt it buck in his hand. He heard the girl's gun roar out beside him and a stream of bullets made a line of dark holes up the metal body of the robot. It stood for a moment, then quivered and Harry heard the roar of its engines. It lifted its axe arm and tried to throw the axe, but the arm suddenly stopped, uplifted. The lights in its eyes faded to dark, but it did not fall.

"You must have short-circuited him," said Harry. "He's dead but he won't lie down."

"They are balanced and have gyroscopic pendulums," the girl said. "They used to be always falling over once until we fitted them with gyroscopes. Now they never fall down until the top stops, some time after they are dead. Go carefully. This is enemy territory,"

They went to the door. The heat was terrific. Opposite, the factory was in flames. The front wall had fallen, or been blown out, and inside Harry could see robots dancing up and down madly in flames—like a crowd of devils in hell. They could not feel the burns, but they seemed afraid of their many intricate wires melting with the heat. They were dancing about trying to find a way out.

"Why don't they dash straight for the street?" he asked.

"They can't see," the girl replied. "Their most intricate mechanism of all is that of sight. It is a series of photoelectric cells which carry vibrationary pictures to their mechanical brain. The mechanical nerves are so fine that they melt easily, so those robots are all blind. See—some have blundered into the street, but they are blind, too."

Harry saw about a score of the robots milling around in the street, bumping into each other and blundering back into the fire. Not having nerve or feeling in their fingertips like humans, it was useless feeling with their hands. The girl raised her gun.

"What are you going to do?" said Harry. "You can't shoot those poor helpless things?"

"Why not?" said the girl. "They are only machines and they can be easily repaired—to kill us. I'll make them harder to repair."

She sent a stream of bullets into one robot and it must have cut some vital part, for the robot leapt up into the air with spasmodic flicks of its legs. Again and again it leapt— then she fired again—at the rear of it, which burst into flames with an explosion.

"The petrol tank is where it sits," she explained. "The gyroscope is dead centre. Those are the parts for which we aim."

"What about the tanks of those in the fire?" Harry asked.

"The tanks are fire-proofed and solidly constructed, but the heat will get to them in time. That is why the robots are so terrified. Look out—this one is not blind."

A robot with gleaming eyes came running funnily round a corner. Behind him followed a small squad. They ran to the blundering, blind robots and passed them from hand to hand down the line away from the fire to safety.

"Let's get out the back way," said the girl.

They turned, but there was no retreating that way. There was a great wall of fire creeping towards them.

At that moment Harry did not know whether he preferred the Professor to whisk him out of this or whether he preferred him to stay with the girl and try and get her out.

He grabbed her hand and they ran out into the street, racing away from the robots towards the darkness. Above the roar and crackle of the flames they heard a tinny, metallic shout and knew that they had been seen.

"How fast can they run?" Harry panted.

"We can run faster," she said, "unless we meet some more or they have a car or machine gun."

A cold shiver chased itself up and down Harry's back and he really began to move then. They turned the first corner and ran down, but half way a car load of robots turned into the street and, in front of the car—which was or a peculiar design—was a thing which Harry knew instinctively was a gun.

Without hesitation he threw himself at a closed glass doorway and he and the girl fell through—the glass flying in all directions.

"Straight through the joint," Harry yelled, wondering whether his throat was cut and whether he would ever be the same man again.

They dashed on through the building, falling over objects in the darkness. "They can catch us out there," the girl gasped. "This way."

She threw open a door, dragged him through, closed the door, pressed a button and they shot upwards with such rapidity that Harry nearly sat down. Then she was opening the door again and dragging him out.

They were on a flat roof. Harry could see clearly in the glare from the many fires and he glanced over himself for cuts. He had none.

"It's a wonder that glass did not cut me," he remarked.

"Glass?" said the girl. "That was not glass—glass belongs to the ancients. We only have it in relics in the museums. That substance you smashed through is a compound made out of wheat. It is like flour with the white colour taken out, refined, made into a paste, drawn out and transparent. It could not cut you. It is very strong and plastic though, and I expected it to throw you back like rubber."

"Popeye, me!" said Harry. "Where do we go from here?"

The girl had drawn a torch from her pocket and she flashed it on. But it had more than any torch Harry had ever seen. It threw a thin beam about half a mile. She pointed it upwards and moved it from side to side as though signalling. She switched it off.

"Here come the robots," she said. "We'll have to hold them off until help comes."

Something flew through the air, upwards from the ground, landed on the roof and rolled to Harry's feet.

"The devils!" she said. "They're using grenades."

Harry bent swiftly, picked up the grenade and hurled it over the roof.

"We used to do that with the Dagoes," he remarked, as there was a huge flash from below and several sheets of metal flashed by. "They'll have some trouble putting that Robert together again."

"Look out," said the girl. "Flatten by the wall."

They threw themselves down close to the low parapet and lay there as a robot-plane swished by, a gun flashing but making no sound. When it had gone over Harry turned to the girl.

"They must have been firing blanks," he said. "No slugs hit the roof."

"It was a ray-gun," the girl replied. "It discharges tremendous bolts of electricity. If one hits you it's like being struck by lightning."

Harry took a deep breath. "There is a happy land, far—far away," he sang softly.

"We have a better gun," said the girl. "See, here comes one of our planes."

The enemy plane was coming back, but straight down out of the sky dropped another plane with an arrangement on the front of it, like a powerful spotlight. This light searched for the other plane and found it, and, as soon as the light touched the plane, it shrivelled and then burst into flame, falling towards the street.

"Phew!" whistled Harry. "That was a hot one."

"It is hot," said the girl. "About five thousand degrees Fahrenheit."

Harry was still whistling when the plane dropped softly down beside them. It was like a large, open launch, had no wings, only narrow stabilisers. Above it gyros twirled on long moveable poles. There was a large propeller and rudder at the rear. They scrambled in and as they dropped on a seat the girl grasped Harry's hand and pressed it to her.

"Don't tell them," she said, "you are a man. Pretend you are a woman and then we need never be separated."

"That's what you think," Harry thought, as colours began to dance before his eyes.

He was sorry, too, because he wanted to see the harbour from above in that year, even at night. But before his mind's eye was an even more intriguing picture. She was a nice girl and there must be thousands like her!

CHAPTER SEVENTEEN —A LICKED DERELICT

When Billy awoke next he found himself in some ruins.

"This place certainly has some ups and downs," he thought. "As I always seem to be in about the same place this would be where the robot factory was, I suppose. If this is it they made a mess of it when they had the last tin-can party."

The ruin was overgrown with creeper, the grass was two or three feet high growing on the piles of rubble. The rocks which had served as the foundations were blackened by fire and time. All the walls were down, the highest piece being no more than eight feet.

He climbed on a piece of rubble and looked over at the harbour. It was deserted! Not a sign of any living thing was to be seen.

He looked towards Sydney, expecting to see the familiar smoke haze of many chimneys. But there was no smoke—nothing but silence. He looked across the water to the farther side. Jungle met his eyes—miles and miles of trees and bushes with here and there a blackened ruin showing through the creepers.

"Lovely!" he murmured to the silence. "No one even to tell me what date it is! Don't tell me they've all wiped each other out! No, that would be a dirty thing to do."

He got up and crossed the ruin carefully until he arrived at what might once have been a street. He pushed his way through the thick vines and bushes, wondering vaguely if there might be any snakes still alive.

He paused for breath at just about the spot where Harry had had his little adventure under the stairs. Billy moved on. A tall tree caught his eye. It looked climbable. From its eminence he might be able to see some signs of life. He began to climb and when he was about forty feet in the air he paused for the tenth time to reconnoitre. This time he was more successful. About a mile off to his left a thin coil of smoke rose lazily in the air.

Ah! thought Billy. Where there's smoke there's fire, and where there's fire there's heat, and where there's heat there's women! Let's go!

He slid down the tree and plunged into the deep scrub. If he had remained another minute and looked towards the harbor he would have seen a strange phenomenon.

Harry suddenly appeared in mid-air over the harbor and, as he fell, he realised that the last time he had vanished he had been in a plane!

He shot down like a bullet and hit the water with hardly a splash!

But one thing at a time. Our business at the moment is with Billy. We will rescue Harry from the water later and continue to wring out his tale, even if it is wet.

It was a cool morning, but Billy soon found himself wet with perspiration. Tearing through that scrub was hard work and he had to be careful he would not lose his direction. But he kept on with it.

Striking a patch of lantana he plunged into it and the spines soon tore his cape to shreds and part of his clothes. He cursed and blundered out. If he had not taken the wrong direction he should be near the fire now.

He pushed his way round a wide tree—and came face to face with a large bear!

At first Billy wondered whether he had been transported to Canada, for he had never heard that grizzly bears were indigenous to Australia. Then he remembered that some time ago animals had acquired speech and reason and had been in control of the earth. In that case there would be Cooks' tourists and other travellers and he supposed the animal kingdom was slightly mixed-up now.

The bear was big enough to eat him and its stare was hostile. Billy swallowed. "Hello!" he said feebly.

The bear kept backing away. "I know what you're up to," it snorted. "You want a fur coat for yourself and you want to kill me and take mine. But I'm not having any, see? You go find yourself a tiger or something. Phooey!"

Then it vanished quickly into the trees. Billy stared after it. Had things become so bad that they had to rob the poor un-dumb animals of their coats? The bear seemed quite indignant—almost cut-up about it, in fact. It could hardly be blamed. So far as that bear was concerned everyone else could go bare.

Billy decided he must have taken the wrong turning somewhere—and then the bear's words came back to him. Tigers! Maybe elephants and all kinds of fauna. Lovely place this Darling Point was getting to be! Quite un-human. Maybe that fire had been set going by a team of rhinoceros or something similar. He would take another tree-top view and get his bearings—without the bears if possible.

There was a large tree nearby and he pushed his way to it and swung himself into the lower branches. He stood upon a branch and reached up for a higher one and looked right into the face of a leopard!

"What's to do?" growled the leopard.

"It's all right," said Billy hastily, "I wasn't going anywhere in particular—I'll go right down again."

"You can have a branch up here if you have anything to pay for rent," the animal said. "This tree belongs to me."

Billy apprehensively watched the leopard lick its lips.

"Very nice tree," he agreed, feeling with his foot for the way down. "Very nice. But I think I prefer somewhere closer to the water if it's all the same to you."

"You can see the water from the top branches," the leopard growled. "Nice hunting tree—plenty of birds come here—and other things which are good eating."

"No doubt!" said Billy, dropping blindly to a lower branch.

He missed it and fell on—hitting the long grass with a thud. The leopard burst into laughter, but Billy did not join in.

He limped away from the tree as fast as he could limp.

CHAPTER EIGHTEEN —MENTAL POISON

"Kids itself it's a Cheshire cat," he grumbled and then stopped dead and sniffed.

He smelt fire. He sniffed again—in the hope he would also smell eggs and bacon and coffee, but no such delectable odour came to him.

There was a small campfire and they were seated round it. At first he thought they were animals, but then he made out that they were women with long hair and wearing rags and animal skins. So that was what the bear had meant. Perhaps they might take his—Billy's—skin to make them a nightie, he mused. In any case, his clothes wouldn't stand a chance. They'd have those off him in a trice and, although Billy was not bashful, he drew the line somewhere.

He decided to watch events for a while and find out how he stood. One of the women shivered. "I'm cold," she growled.

"Don't whinge, Sharpsnout," another said. "Aren't we all cold? The only thing that could warm us is a man—but where is one?"

"I thought I knew, Brittlebottom," said the third woman, who was lying to one side and seemed to be in pain. "But he must have moved or been snavelled. Our blood has been thinned over the centuries. We haven't had enough meat, that's what it is."

"The Fifth Glacial Period is upon us," said Sharpsnout. "We can never survive without Man. You told us, Draggledrawers, that you knew where there was one—and led us on a wild goose chase."

"Wild man chase," corrected Brittlebottom.

Draggledrawers moved painfully and moaned a trifle. "And then," she said slowly, "while I slept last night I was knifed in the back!"

The other two stared at the fire. "I can't understand how that happened," said Sharpsnout.

"Perhaps it was the man," suggested Brittlebottom.

"Maybe!" said Draggledrawers bitterly.

"You can't blame us," winged Sharpsnout. "We are your closest friends."

"CLOSE is the right word," snarled Draggledrawers. "You wouldn't lend me a handful of cold water."

"Aw, take off your hat!" snapped Brittlebottom.

"What hat?"

"The one you're talking through."

"Now, don't get arguing, girls," said Sharpsnout hastily. "Let's drink the last of the whisky."

Billy nearly fell over. He could not believe his ears. Whisky? It didn't seem possible. His mouth watered. He watched Draggledrawers pull an earthen bottle from beneath her and hand it to Sharpsnout. He couldn't stand it any longer. He flung off his coat and waistcoat.

"Here's a go!" said Sharpsnout and placed the bottle to her lips. Billy was preparing to dash in. The bottle was passed to Brittlebottom, who took a swig. Billy looked at his shoes. He still did not look in the mode. He would just walk up casually and say, "Howdy, girls, just having a little snifter. Yes, I don't mind if I do."

His thoughts were interrupted by a roar of mad laughter from Draggledrawers. She had been handed the bottle for her drink, but she had not drunk. Billy wondered if she had gone into the horrors in anticipation. He decided to wait a moment.

"Why the attack of the giggles?" Sharpsnout asked. "I can't see anything funny and you haven't had your drink yet."

Draggledrawers leant forward dramatically. "I can see something funny!" she hissed. "Last night, while I lay asleep, one of you two crept upon me and stabbed me. Oh, you needn't deny it—I know! I did not lose consciousness after the blow and I saw a dim figure skulking away, but I could not be sure which one of you it was. I could not call out in case the killer came back to finish the job—and me."

"That—that's ridiculous." said Sharpsnout. "What would either of us want to kill you for?"

"Because there wasn't enough food for three—there wasn't enough whisky, there wasn't enough clothes—and if you found a man, there would be one less to share him with.

After a while the killer would have removed the last rival. Well, if I go you'll go with me. To-day I poisoned the whisky!"

Sharpsnout broke out all in a dither. She stared for a moment, then got a strangle-hold on her throat and jumped to her feet. Brittlebottom did not move, but her eyes were fixed on Draggledrawers with fear and hate.

"You swine!" she said.

Draggledrawers chuckled softly. "You have only a few moments to live," she said.

The two who had drunk the whisky were staring in horror-struck fashion at Draggledrawers.

"Why should you kill an innocent woman with the guilty?" moaned Sharpsnout.

"Well, I don't want to do that," said Draggledrawers, pulling a smaller earthen flask from beneath her. "In this flask is an antidote—for one only. Settle it amongst yourselves."

She placed the bottle down between the two women and they stared into each other's eyes.

"Let's toss?" said Sharpsnout gently.

"No," said Brittlebottom harshly. "I want to live!"

She swept up the flask, placed it to her lips and quickly drained it in three gulps. Then, pulling a wry face, she sprang back like an animal at bay, drawing a dagger from some hidden spot in her clothing.

"Now!" she snarled. "Sharpsnout will die from the poison—and you, Draggledrawers, will die from this knife. I failed last time, but I will make no mistake now."

Draggledrawers tipped back her head and laughed heartily. Then she raised the whisky bottle.

"Here's how!" she said and took a deep drink.

The others stared at her.

"Then—then," Sharpsnout burbled, "it wasn't poisoned after all?"

"Not likely," said Draggledrawers. "I wouldn't poison good whisky for anyone—especially this stuff we found in that ancient city and which is about two thousand years old. But I wanted to find the coward who knifed me in the back. Once a coward, always a coward! So I laid my trap. No, the whisky wasn't poisoned. But the antidote—that was different!"

Brittlebottom stared at her taunter, felt at her throat and muttered. Then she clasped her stomach—her eyes wide with fear. She turned and plunged into the forest and they listened to her crashing through the scrub until no sound could be heard.

Sharpsnout climbed a stump and peered after her.

"She has gone deep into the forest," she said. "Deeper and deeper. I'm sorry you did it that way."

"And what that forest gets it keeps!" said Draggledrawers with grim satisfaction. "I hope she gets a new fur coat—which is still alive!"

Sharpsnout turned back to her. "What was the poison?" she asked.

"It wasn't," said Draggledrawers. "It was only mental poison. She has taken a good dose of Epsom salts. That'll fix her!"

Billy swallowed, and moved quietly away through the trees in search of a kind tiger.

CHAPTER NINETEEN —CAVE!

Harry went down a long way and, in the excitement and the shock of the cold water, he released the gun he still carried. He was sorry for that later. It would have been a nice memento. When—and if—he got back, it would be useless dragging the harbor for it, for it wouldn't be there in 1945.

He swam upwards, hampered by his clothes, and hoped he would come up near some craft which would not contain enemies in the shape of animals or tin men.

Harry was a strong swimmer and shortly he was hauling himself up some rocks. He lay down in the sun to get his breath. In the meantime he looked about him. Everywhere was desolation, but off to his left a trifle, were some deep caves in a low cliff. He would make for those later.

Having recovered his breath he rose and stripped off his clothes. There did not seem any need to wear them here, as there was no one to see. He wrung them out and spread them over a big rock to dry. By constantly shaking the cape he got that dry first and he twisted it into a loin cloth. Then he made for the caves—going quietly and keeping out a wary eye for wild animals, tin men, wild women or what have you. As he neared the caves he heard a voice. It was a soft feminine voice. He dropped on all fours and crept closer. This might be a large female cat, for all he knew. He had no wish to meet a large, and maybe wild, pussy —he was not dressed for it.

He drew up to near the entrance of the cave and then he could hear the voice plainly. It was talking uninterruptedly as though in self-communication. Harry peeped round the corner of the cave-entrance. A large, handsome girl was sitting in the centre, drawing lines on the sand with a stick. She had a small leopard skin round her waist, and nothing else. It struck Harry that Taronga Park used to be near here somewhere [*Taronga Park is Sydney's zoo – Ed.*]. Maybe this was one of its caves—still inhabited by something similar to an animal.

There was no one else in the cave, so he rose to his feet and strolled in, his arms folded. The girl looked up as he entered. He was still attired in the cape-loin-cloth and his folded arms covered his chest. She took him for a woman.

"Hello, stranger," she said. "Where do you come from?"

"I have come a long way," said Harry, leaning on a shady portion of the wall. "What year is this?"

The girl went lackadaisically back to drawing a man in the sand.

"The year four thousand, of course," she said.

"I must be getting up speed," Harry remarked. "I suppose I'm what you'd call a fast man."

The girl looked up. "What did you say about a man?" she asked with interest. "Have you seen one anywhere? Would you care to share him?"

"I suppose I look like a Pansy," Harry said. "It's a wonder the voice—but that water was pretty cold and maybe my tones have risen a little."

"Strongarm and Ironhead have gone hunting for a man and to see if the man-traps are set. Oh, I hope they catch one—though I don't suppose they will—men are so scarce nowadays. I wish I had one."

"Don't I look like a man?" asked Harry.

The girl looked at him and shook her head. "No," she said, "you are not feminine enough."

"Well, I FEEL like a man."

"Do you?" the girl asked. "How does a man feel?"

"Lots of ways," said Harry, as he unfolded his arms and let his hands drop. "Look at me."

The girl looked up again and for a moment her eyes were on his face, puzzled. She was about to ask "Why?" when her glance dropped to his chest and stayed.

"It can't be!" she breathed.

"It is," said Harry. "I would have been feminine if I hadn't been born a couple of thousand years ago. Look me over—masculine to the finger-tips—and how! One of the old brigade—the old vintage—stamped on the bottle 1917."

She slowly backed round him to cut off any retreat he might make through the entrance.

"You really are a man!" she said. "Oh, how perfectly marvellous! Now I can have children and everything! Don't struggle with me, please—let me make love to you."

"What is your name?"

"Softarms!" she said, coming closer.

"Well, Softarms," said Harry, "we did things differently in my day. Then men were on top, though—now I come to think of it—women really did do most of the love-making. But I'll meet you half-way. My name is Bulls-whiskers."

He took the girl roughly in his arms, tilted her face back and kissed her—a long kiss with every trimming he had. When he paused for breath the girl closed her eyes and sighed gustily.

"Ooooh—that was heaven! I have found a man! I hope they don't take you from me!"

"They?" asked Harry. "Who's they?"

"The other women. Oh, I must hide you before Strong-arm sees you. She will grab you for herself. Let us take to the bush."

"That would only be jumping from bush to bush and I haven't any boots on," Harry said. "I'll handle her."

"You won't. She is like her name—Strongarm. They call me Softarms because they say I am soft like the women used to be in the twentieth century."

"That's how I like 'em," Harry said. "I was trained on that kind—and they aren't so soft at that. They dressed differently to you, though that thing you wear is far nicer. It hasn't got any hooks on it, but I'll bet it would have had a few eyes round it in my time."

"Strongarm is our leader and most manly," said Softarms, anxiously looking over her shoulder at the entrance. "She grabs all the men and carries them off to her cave."

"She can't be so very manly, then. She must have something feminine about her. Let us sit down." He dropped down on the sand and she snuggled near to him, trying to pull him closer. As Harry dropped down he sat on something and, feeling around, he found it was his cigarette case with lighter attached, which he had placed in the cape pocket. He drew it out. The contents seemed perfectly dry. The girl watched him carefully.

He put a cigarette in his mouth and lit it from the lighter. He took a deep inhalation and blew out the smoke. The girl started back.

"Oh, oh!" she gasped. "You're on fire—in your mouth. Your stomach's on fire!"

"No. My blood might run hot at times but it's never that bad. Haven't you ever heard of cigarettes?"

The girl was thoughtful a moment. "Oh yes," she said at last. "They say there used to be such things. They called it smoking, didn't they? Women started with cigarettes and then tried pipes and cigars, but, because they could never really handle any of them, they prohibited smoking when they got to power, though sly-smoking went on for some time. Let me try."

She climbed on to his lap and sat on his legs.

"Wait a moment," said Harry, wincing, "you are sitting on my—my cigarette case. That's better."

He placed the cigarette in her mouth and she took a deep draw; then burst into a fit of coughing and he slapped her on the bare back.

"Take it away," she gasped. "It is awful. Darling, I don't like smoking, so you will have to give it up."

"The same old gag," said Harry. "Well, there's no harm in telling me—even if I take no notice. We never did."

"But I say you have to," said Softarms firmly.

"And I say I won't," said Harry. "As I am a caveman now, my word goes around here."

She stared at him for a moment, then smiled. "Wonderful!" she breathed. "Let me love you."

"Not so fast!" said Harry. "I had a busy night last night. Wait until I've got my breath."

"Last night?" said the girl. "Where were you last night?"

"Did I say last night? I meant last night two—three centuries ago."

The girl leapt to her feet. "Sssh!" she hissed. "I can hear someone coming. Quick—I must hide you!"

CHAPTER TWENTY —CLUBS ARE THUMPS!

She jerked him to his feet and ran him up the cave to where a large rock stood near the far end. She pushed him behind this and walked quickly back down the cave, dropped on the ground and began drawing pictures with her stick again.

In a moment two women entered the cave. Both were bigger than Softarms—large and muscly. They also wore only skins about their loins and one of them carried a large knobby club. They were handsome enough, but very masculine in their walk, voice and demeanour.

"Hi, there Softarms!" cried the one with the club in a voice which echoed round the cave.

"Hi there, Strongarm," Softarms replied. "Did you have —er—any luck?"

"Not a sign of a man—not a track—not even his tail feathers," said Strongarm, then lifted her head and sniffed. "What's burning round here? Where's the fire? That's a peculiar smell. What have you been doing, Softarms?"

"Er—nothing, good chief Strongarm," Softarms replied, rising fearfully to her feet.

"It smells like a new perfume," said the third woman, Ironhead, "and only men use perfume. Perhaps she has found a man!"

Strongarm grasped Softarms by the wrist. "Have you found a man?" she thundered.

"Er—yes—no—he's—"

Strongarm cast her aside and stared round the cave. She spied a wisp of smoke curling up from behind the rock.

"Where's that smoke coming from? Have you built a fire round there?" She walked up to the rock and looked round it at Harry. "Aha! What have we here?"

Harry gave a sickly grin. "Hyar?" he said.

"It's a man!" Strongarm exulted and Ironhead ran to see. "Come out, you beauty!"

"Looks as though I'm going to suffer a fate worse than death!" Harry remarked, as he was dragged forth by the arm.

Softarms ran to them. "He's mine!" she yelled. "I saw him first!"

She grabbed his other arm and tried to drag him away.

"Hoy! Hoy!" said Harry. "Break that down! If you split me in two parts I won't be a bit of good. Don't let's argue. I'm hers—she saw me first."

"Shut up, toy!" Strongarm growled. "You will be MY plaything and no one else's."

"What about me?" grunted Ironhead, looking him over with covetous eyes while she stroked her chin. "Haven't I served you well, Strongarm? Didn't we promise to share anything we caught?"

"I hope they don't decide to divide the spoils," Harry mused.

"But it was ME who caught him," screamed Softarms. "Finding's keepings!"

"All right," said Strongarm craftily. "We all have a claim, so the easiest way to decide is to fight it out with clubs to see who gets him."

"Hey!" said Harry, "That's not fair to the little one!"

"You shut up and mind your own business," snapped Strongarm.

"Well, I seem to have a slight interest in this affair," remarked Harry, "so that it IS my business—and I'm likely to be a very busy man."

Strongarm pushed him up towards the top end of the cave and went to a corner where stood two piles of clubs.

"Soft clubs?" she asked and the others nodded, although the clubs did not look too soft to Harry. "Three knockdowns is out."

The chief doled out a club to each and the women stood in a triangle.

"Ready? Fight!" she said, and immediately konked Softarms on the skull. The clubs were springy. Softarms sat down with a bump. Before Strongarms could recover from her swing she received a clout from Ironhead which knocked her to her knees. By that time Softarms was up again, and with a round-arm swing, her club took Ironhead on the back of the thing she was named after and she went through the air in a somersault. Harry decided this sort of thing had gone far enough.

He dashed into the fray just in time to intercept a blow being sent from Strongarm to Softarms with thanks, and he sat down with a bump and a headache.

"Never fear!" he murmured to himself. "Tobruk was worse than this. Up guards and at 'em."

The fight had stopped for a moment—the three women staring at him. He bounced up and tore Strongarm's club from her hand—then he dashed at Ironhead and grabbed her club and threw it away. Next he ripped away Softarm's club and threw it out of the cave mouth.

"Now, look here!" he snapped. "I've had enough of this—and you've given me a headache like a hangover. You'll be really hurting someone if you keep this up. Now, understand this, girls—Man has come back into his own again. Remember I'm boss here from now on and there'll be no hanky panky. You sit there, Strongarm."

He pointed to a spot on the sand. Strongarm drew herself up. "You're mad!" she said. Harry raised the club. "You wouldn't dare. I won't."

Harry, remembering his headache, hit her so hard across the shoulders she rolled five yards. As she staggered to all fours the club caught her on the most accessible place and she shot into a heap at the very spot he had indicated.

"Holed out in one," he remarked, as he stood over her. "Don't say won't to me."

She stared up at him with amazed and adoring eyes. "O.K., dear," she said. "O.K."

Harry threw out his chest so that his loin cloth slipped down about six inches.

"That's the stuff to give 'em," he said, hitching it up again. "I'll show 'em what I've got." He turned suddenly on Ironhead. "You sit over there."

"I won't be bossed by you," said Ironhead scornfully. "I'll show fight. No man can—"

His club took her in the small of the back and when she stopped rolling she crawled to the position he had indicated.

"Who did you say was boss?" asked Harry truculently.

"You are, lovely one," she sighed ecstatically. "I am your slave."

CHAPTER TWENTY-ONE —A LONG FAST

Harry took a few strutting turns round the cave, the women watching him with dog-like eyes.

"This is a cop!" he said. "I knew Man would finish on top, but I didn't think it would be me would start the ball rolling. You, Softarms, can sit here."

She lowered herself to the sand where he pointed and them he sat down, the club across his knees and the women grouped before him. He looked into the three adoring faces and grinned. The women drew a few inches nearer.

"I don't know where to start first," Harry said. "Maybe we had better draw lots. This beats 1945 to a frazzle, I always knew the ancient Turks had the right idea. I wonder how many more women are roaming about waiting to be tamed. Now if that Professor joker will only let me stop here for a week or so I might be able to leave a few memories. That reminds me—I wonder if any of these girls are related to me. That girl in the air-raid—woof!"

The last exclamation was caused by the three girls springing on him together. They had become impatient! He was being smothered under a barrage of kisses, when the women paused and sprang up as a cry came from the cave's mouth.

Harry looked in that direction. Crowded there were about thirty women and they were all looking at him with hungry eyes. He leapt to his feet and his loin-cloth, loosened in the struggle, dropped round his feet.

"Wow!" he said, grabbing it. "This is too much for little me. I've changed my mind—" The new arrivals rushed into the cave, screaming war cries and "Tally—ho". Then they paused.

Their quarry had vanished!

* * *

The great gong had gone and the guests were assembled in the ballroom again.

Dawn was just breaking over the harbor. I had been standing at the window watching it. It was beautiful. It began at 4.15 by spreading a stealthily grey cloak over everything. The birds stirred in the garden and, as the light grew, one chirped—then another and another. One by one they all joined in and then the doves set up a steady chorus.

Then the gong clanged and we all went back to the ballroom, to witness the finish of the experiment. Personally I was a little dubious as to whether we would ever see Harry and Billy again.

The Professor had not left the stage. Through the hours he had been whirling his instruments and shooting the two men through time.

"Ladies and gentlemen," he said to the yawning guests. "You will now see the time-travellers again and they should have a story to tell us. They may even be changed. Watch!"

All eyes turned on the cylinders as the Professor bent over his instruments. Sparks and colour leapt up in them—then into one of them appeared Billy—still dressed in his evening suit with the addition of a cape. The suit and cape were much damaged. He opened his eyes and took a quick, apprehensive glance round, and one of the Professor's assistants stepped to the cylinder, opened the door and led him out. He stood staring.

The other cylinder glowed and coloured—then Harry appeared. Women screamed—for Harry was perfectly nude. In one hand he carried what appeared to be a cape and, in the other, a wooden club. He also stared apprehensively—then the Professor's assistants rushed the cylinder, opened the door, threw a long coat round him and drew him forth, standing him beside Billy. The room was silent now, waiting for their first words.

"Where are we this time?" asked Harry.

"We seem to be back where we started," said Billy.

"What happened to you—were you telling some dame a bedtime story with a club?"

"No—but I've lost my clothes and damn near everything else."

The Professor switched off all his gadgets and went up to them.

"Well, gentlemen," he said. "You seem to have been having some adventures. That club—how old is it?"

"That club," said Harry, "is minus two thousand odd years. I don't know whether I should kick you or kiss you—though some of it was good fun. I just lost my suit and a harem."

"Where have you been?" asked the Professor.

"Seeing various girl friends," said Harry, "but they won't be born for a long time yet and I can't wait."

"Why worry?" said Billy looking over the crowd. "Who wants to make love to a microbe when there's all these lovelies right here. Why not have one of their ancestors?"

"Good idea!" Harry said, staring at the crowd. Then he exclaimed sharply. "What do you know about that—there's a girl dead ring of Softarms."

I was standing by his elbow. "That is not her name," I said. "That is Miss Featherwing, the noted feminist."

Harry nodded. "I've just been making love to her granddaughter—one hundred times removed. Now if I were to marry this Featherwing dame—why, Softarms might have been one of my descendants, too. This doesn't bear thinking about."

"Harry," I said, as the ballroom started to empty again, "I am here to offer you one hundred pounds for the exclusive rights of the story of your time-trip. If you are agreeable you can sign the rights over to me straight away."

"A hundred quid?" said Harry, staring at me.

"Isn't it enough?"

"Too right. Wait till I tell Billy."

We looked round for Billy, but he was making his way as fast as he could for the bar and supper room. He had just remembered he had not eaten or drunk for two thousand years!

The End

ABOUT THE AUTHOR

Paul de Wreder is the pseudonym of John Winton Heming, an Australian author whose principal work spans the 1930s and 1940s. J.W. Heming is more accurately described as a pulp writer than a science fiction writer. He wrote straight adventure, mysteries and detective tales, even romances, all under a variety of pen names.

AFTERWORD

Billy Stewart and Harry Nash are two Australian war veterans, down on their luck at the close of World War II (accurately predicted to end in 1945). They are lured by Professor Slagoscar to his home in the upscale Sydney suburb of Darling Point on the pretext of a dinner party. The promise of free food and booze and the company of society ladies is too much for the friends to resist.

They are drugged and placed in the cubicles of a time projector. The Professor succeeds in sending his unwitting guinea pigs forwards in time. A short stay in each era enables the friends to get into all kinds of scrapes and dangers – and hopefully gets them out again.

The story, light-weight romp that it is, nevertheless reminded me of H.G. Wells' classic novelette that started it all—*The Time Machine*. The strong sense of place and its changes over epochs of deep time that is a hallmark of Wells' story is also present in *Time Marches Off*. Sydney Harbour is viewed through succeeding cycles of development and destruction.

Time Marches Off is not great literature. Unlike Wells, who always applied his intellect to the problems he foresaw in his own day and in humanity's future, J.W. Heming was writing merely to amuse and entertain.

Even though it's played strictly for laughs, *Time Marches Off* manages a number of surprising prophecies from its vantage point of 1942—real predictions of the social and sexual morés of future cultures and the technologies that serve them.

The era of the sexual revolution is followed by the age of metrosexuals and the uneasy gender equality is followed by the subjugation of men. The masculinisation of women and feminisation of men may have been a send-up of wartime working women, an issue contemporary to the book's publication. In 2014 however, we definitely live in the era of the gender-blenders.

Heming takes a further look into the darker side of radical feminism by showing an oppressive *female* patriarchy. Genetic engineering ensures that fewer boys are born than girls and the scarce male population is segregated from society, largely into stud-farms.

Once the age of robots becomes a reality, android workers and husbands become popular. In an anticipation of the kind of realistic sex dolls now coming out of Japan, Heming slyly points out that robot husbands are more expensive than the simpler worker/handyman models because they have more functions and come with attachments... The slogan of Brass and Company - Robot Manufacturers. "You Always Can With a B-Co. Man," is another hint at these possibilities.

Genetic engineering also brings intelligence to animals, anticipating Clifford Simak's immortal *City* series of stories. Unlike this classic anthology, Heming's intelligent animals rebel from their creators' rule and develop a taste for human flesh in the bargain. In a parable for our time of

Genetically Modified Organisms, Heming shows how science without wisdom always leads to unwanted consequences.

Surveillance drones, a New World Order, life extension, video-phones, anti-individualism, sexbots, artificial intelligence, genetic engineering, a series of Great Depressions, rocketships and ray guns; standard science fiction paraphernalia are here but with compelling additions relevant to our own times.

With all these heavy subjects, you would think that this is a serious book. Nothing could be further from the truth. The humour is dry and very Australian and the gags and wry observations keep on coming.

Like the best satire, *Time Marches Off* holds a mirror to our own society and makes you laugh at the same time. Even though it first appeared over 70 years ago, it's still relevant enough to comment on our times today.

Igor Spajic

Sydney, Australia

December 2014

Paul deWreder